CRISES IN KERRVILLE

A JAN KOKK MYSTERY

ROY F. SULLIVAN

authorHOUSE®

AuthorHouse™
1663 Liberty Drive
Bloomington, IN 47403
www.authorhouse.com
Phone: 1-800-839-8640

Published by AuthorHouse 12/05/2014

ISBN: 978-1-4969-5673-6 (sc)
ISBN: 978-1-4969-5674-3 (e)

TO NANCY: EDITOR-IN-CHIEF, KEEPER

OTHER BOOKS BY THE AUTHOR

Roy F. Sullivan:
Scattered Graves: The Civil War Campaigns of Confederate Brigadier General and Cherokee Chief Stand Watie

The Civil War in Texas and the Southwest

The Texas Navies

The Texas Revolution: Tejano Heroes

Escape from Phnom Penh: Americans in the Cambodian War

Escape from the Pentagon

RF Sullivan:
A Jan Kokk Mystery: The Curacao Connection

A Jan Kokk Mystery: Murder Cruises the Antilles

A Jan Kokk Mystery: Gambol in Vegas

A Jan Kokk Mystery: Murder by the Dozen

ABOUT THE AUTHOR

Happily retired from the U.S. Army and U.S. State Department, Roy Sullivan spends his time imagining what famous Curacao investigator Jan Kokk is doing to whom, why and where.

When last seen, Kokk was solving murders off Little Corn Island near Nicaragua (see "Murder by the Dozen"). Invited to Texas several times, Kokk always has other fish to fry.

Until now, this time it's different. During Kokk's flight over Texas to Los Angeles, a bomb threat and murder cause an emergency landing.

Where else? In Texas!

Kokk, the trained crime observer, provides the FBI, Texas Rangers and County Sheriff's Department his eyewitness and expert advice on the two crimes: the bomb threat and murder. Janie an attractive flight attendant, lavishes attention on Kokk while he tries to solve the crimes. Will Kokk share eventual answers to 'who dun it' with the phalanx of lawmen if it involves his new lady?

Author's Note: If you're unfamiliar with Texas geography, the Hill Country encompasses twenty-five counties nestled in the approximate center of Texas. The Hill Country extends westward from Austin, the state capital, then to Kerrville where this story takes place. From Kerrville the Hill Country extends farther to Ozona and Big Lake on its western side.

MEET THE MAJOR FICTIONAL CHARACTERS HEREIN, IN ORDER OF THEIR APPEARANCE

Janie Roland.   Lively airline attendant searching for her Mr. Perfect.

Ann.   Janie's co-worker, friend and advisor.

Louisa.   Head attendant on Flt 236. The boss of Janie and Ann.

Roger Twist.   Famed Hollywood film maker and multimillionaire.

Robert House.   Twist's "go-fer" or manservant.

Babbs Solomon.   Twist's personal secretary who blames Twist for firing her cousin.

Harold Moon.   Long-time collaborator with Twist on Hollywood productions. Holds Twist responsible for his wife's death.

Perry.   Twist's tax advisor. Skilled in accounting loopholes.

Gloria Denham.   Curvaceous starlet pursuing a leading role in Twist's next bombshell movie.

Oliver.   Twist's paid movie reviewer.

Jan Kokk.   Famed PI from Curacao on a job for his government to return a diplomat home from Los Angeles. His airplane is forced to land in Kerrville, Texas.

Police Commissioner Felix van Hooser.   Kokk's friend and Chief of Curacao Police.

Captain Bringuel.   Pilot of Flt 236 forced to make an emergency landing in Kerrville.

First Officer Benson.   Copilot of Flt 236.

Jane Spellman.   Radio operator at Kerrville-Kerr County Airport who responds to the emergency call from Flt 236.

Bob Mitchell.   Manager of the Kerrville-Kerr County Airport where Flt 236 makes an emergency landing.

Sheriff Swartz.   Tough Kerr County sheriff.

Dr. Harrell.   County Medical Examiner.

Texas Ranger Captain Hooks.   Assumes responsiblity of investigation from Swartz. Supports Kokk's observations.

George Aspinwall.   Manager of Kerrville's YO Ranch Resort Hotel.

Agent-in-Charge Westbrook.   Heads the FBI team with overall responsibility for the investigation.

Deputy John Rabe.   Offers Kokk a ride to the YO Hotel despite Sheriff Swartz.

Special Agent Korf.   Investigator on the FBI team.

Dan Roe.   Represents Homeland Security Department in the investigation.

Mike Kirby. TV commentator for San Antonio's WOAI.

Special Agent Daniels. FBI interviewer of female suspects. Follows up on a lead from Kokk.

Fred Reed. Airlines official from Dallas sent to placate Flt 236 passengers.

Johan Piaker. Curacao's Consul General in Los Angeles.

Henri Boudin. Piaker's administrative officer.

Judy. Secretary of the Los Angeles Consulate.

ONE

"Quit wriggling, Janie! Or those security guys at the gate will stop us and make us late for our check-in."

Out-of-breath, frosted auburn-hair Ann blinked hazel eyes at her younger companion. Ann's pageboy cut shook with emphasis, exaggerating her tallness.

Close friends sometimes kidded Ann about being so slim. The refrain of one oft-repeated song went

"She ain't skinny,
She's tall,
That's all!"

Ann softened her reproach. "You know Big Bad Louisa is the lead attendant today on our flight to Los Angeles?"

Janie stopped abruptly to face her friend. "Why in the world would security stop us?"

The two airline attendants dressed in snappy uniforms, caps and high heels enjoyed the attention of all the males sharing their corridor in Miami International Airport's terminal 5.

The two friends epitomized their airline and its rigorous training. One brunette, the other auburn, they oozed confidence and elegance as they hurried through the staring crowds.

"To frisk **you**," Ann pointed a manicured finger at her younger partner. "Probably with a full body scan. They'll want to know if your jiggle is flesh or false.

"So…just walk naturally. Okay?"

Curly-trussed Janie blinked up at Ann. "Girl friend, I suppose you don't wiggle a bit, too?"

Ann sighed. "Once I did. But I've got more hours on my airframe than that 737 we're about to board for Los Angeles.

"C'mon. We've got to hustle to make it to gate 45 in time to avoid Louisa's chewing us out in front of all the others. I hate it when she does that!"

"Whoa!" Janie held up her free hand. "Stop that shuttle!"

She smiled, waving at the young male driving an electric cart. "Gate 45, please. And hurry."

Grappling with their wheeled luggage, the two young women in tailored blue and taupe uniforms, climbed aboard the halted cart.

Dismayed by the females' quick getaway, a nearby cluster of battle dress-clad soldiers waved goodbye and blew them kisses.

The crowds thronging the corridors and waiting areas of terminal 5 seemed to part like water as the driver continually rang the cart bell while speeding toward the far gate.

Placing a reassuring hand on her uniform cap, green-eyed Janie used the other to tug at the short skirt straddling the carry-on chafing her knees.

Ann leaned back, straightening the silver barrette in her hair. "Looks like we'll make it," she breathed in relief as their cart stopped in front of gate 45.

Once off, they thanked the driver, then quickened their staccato pace toward the entrance to Flight 236. High heels clicking on the polished corridor, they dragged carry-ons behind them, flashing smiles at the impatient passengers already queuing at the gate.

Once aboard the gleaming Boeing 737 aircraft, they pushed their luggage into bins and nodded at the other three attendants. They joined the cluster of females being briefed by Louisa.

"Where are our male attendants?" Ann asked.

"Well, lookie, ladies." Louisa eyed the newly arrived pair. "Our *Hot in Cleveland* look-alikes finally have joined us."

Irritated, Louisa crinkled her nose at Ann and Janie. "I've already covered the cockpit crew and special assignments for today's flight to LA.

"We're it, ladies." Louisa returned to Ann's question "The reason there are no males among us is my next topic. Our passengers are boarding soon, so pay attention.

"We received a most unusual request from the apparently very wealthy passenger reserving **all** twelve first class seats for his party of seven. No male attendants, he specified."

"I bet those seven first classers are all male," Janie batted eyelids while nudging Ann."

Her instructions interrupted, Louisa glared at Janie. "Wrong, again. Two of the seven in first class are female.

"You're wanting to know who or what is this wealthy passenger?" Louisa paused to correct the scarf of the attendant next to her.

"He's Mr. Big to us. He's just returning from Brazil's Sao Paulo film festival and now on his way with his merry band of Hollywooders back to California. I expect you all to be especially hospitable to Mr. Big and the group of movie types surrounding him in first class."

"What's his name?" asked the attendant whose scarf had been smoothed.

Louisa glanced at her manifest. "Mr. Roger Twist, a very wealthy Hollywood executive. Even owns his own studio. You are expected to unleash on him all that charm learned during attendant training.

"Don't screw up my retirement plans or I'll be very unhappy." She surveyed every face, her frown deepening at Janie.

Louisa tossed her short, graying bobbed hair, stifling a yawn. "Today we've got nearly a full load in both the economy plus and economy sections."

Despite Louisa's frown, Janie ventured, "Who works first class?"

"Only seven people seated there." Louisa winked. "Guess I'll have to handle them all by myself."

Hastily she added, "But I'll be helping you out in economy, too, of course."

"Here they come," another attendant warned as passengers began tramping up the long incline ramp toward the aircraft's open door.

"Smile, ladies! Big smile!" intoned Louisa.

"Here we go," Janie said glumly, turning toward the back of the aircraft. "I knew I'd get cattle car duty again. Did you see that look Louisa gave me?" Playfully, she punched Ann on the shoulder."

"Relax, kid. Relax," Ann advised her friend.

"Maybe you'll meet Mr. Perfect today!" Ann nudged Janie toward the rear.

"Even in the economy section!" she added.

TWO

The 737 took off smoothly at noon and lifted high above greater Miami, heading west toward the Texas coast. There it would change to a new bearing for Los Angeles.

Captain Bringuel in the cockpit barely had turned off the seat belt sign. At the same moment, Louisa received a surprise visitor to her forward starboard galley. She almost dropped the microphone to announce that the seat belt sign had been turned off.

"Sir," was her automatic response to the intruder, "Please be seated. Our beverage service will begin shortly."

It was the same young man whom she'd noticed hanging up Mr. Twist's dark suit coat. Now he wore a red waiter's jacket with small silver buttons over a gleaming white shirt and a spiffy black bow tie.

The man regarded her with a smile. "I'm Robert, Mr. Twist's factotum," he began.

"I'm here to serve Mr. Twist—and of course his party—of which I've just made a seating chart for your convenience." He thrust a drawing into Louisa's free hand.

"Robert," he repeated with a small bow. "At your service, Miss…"

"I'm Louisa, chief flight attendant," she replied, aplomb returning after her initial surprise. She inspected the brash, red-jacketed young man attempting to usurp her responsibilities.

"If you'll just resume your seat, sir. I'll be right with you." Uncertainly she examined the seating chart handed her. It indicated Twist's seat number as well as that of each of his party occupying the entirety of the first class section.

"You don't understand, Louisa--that's indeed a charming name." Robert bestowed a toothy smile.

"I'm employed by Mr. Twist to see to his personal needs. I'll require one of your two forward galleys to prepare refreshments and meals for Mr. Twist and his guests. I'm relieving you of all such duties."

He planted a crisp bill in her blouse pocket. "Now do you understand?"

Robert looked about the miniscule galley with distaste. "This one will have to do. With your kind permission, I'll begin preparing drinks for Mr. Twist and his party using your liquor stock. He likes a vodka martini and canapes prior to a light lunch."

He reached into the overhead and removed two large leather covered squares that looked like pizza delivery boxes. "Here are the cheese puffs I brought aboard for him."

He blinked. "My, my. No fresh limes? You **do** have a vodka suitable for martinis? Maybe *Grey Goose?* Mr. Twist likes his martinis with a twist, of course," Robert chuckled.

Despite the intensity of his monologue, Robert paused to tweak a small piece of lint from Louisa's blouse.

"By the way," he smiled again as if she were a slow learner. "What's on today's menu for luncheon?"

Despite fifteen years as an attendant, this was a baffling and outrageous experience for Louisa. She almost bit her lip but managed a reply.

"First class has a choice of a souffle or shrimp salad," she mumbled, mesmerized by the overload of information and the printed seating chart handed her.

Robert raised his eyebrows in anticipation. "And a choice of white wines?"

"Well, yes," she managed. "A choice of chardonnay or chardonnay," she quipped, trying to regain control.

Robert grimaced. "That will have to do."

He motioned her out of the galley. "Now, shoo, shoo. I must get busy.

"And please tell your ladies to refrain from using this galley for the duration of the flight."

He studied his polished nails. "Oh, one other thing, dear Louisa. I'm sure Mr. Twist will be very pleased by your cooperative attitude. So pleased that he may pen a note to your airlines president conveying appreciation for the splendid efforts of you and your team."

With a forced smile, he closed the galley curtain in her face.

Anger barely controlled, Louisa closed her eyes, remembering her mother's admonition to count to ten before acting from rage. Numbly, she stared at the seating chart once she'd counted to ten. Twice.

She made a quick stop in the forward port rest room to stare at her reflection in the mirror and renew lip-gloss. Sighing, she examined the crisp bill Robert had slid into her pocket. It was $100.

Thinking about early retirement, she strolled through the first class compartment, smiling and nodding at the new passengers, offering magazines and small pillows.

She easily identified 'Mr. Big' in his second row, aisle seat. At least fifty, she estimated, his hair was a carefully tousled gray. He wore a tailored vest and trousers, silk tie and elaborate gold links. Beside him, seat A2 was vacant except for a pile of loose papers and folders all marked "Urgent."

Roger Twist returned a cell phone to the middle-aged female sitting directly in front of him. Louisa guessed from the conservative dress, manner and 70's hair style, that the woman was Twist's personal secretary. Her name on the chart, occupying seat B1, was listed simply as 'Babbs.'

The florid Mr. Twist continued an animated conversation with the man seated across the aisle in seat E2. The man leaned over the aisle toward Twist, thumping a thick script with his hand. From flowered shirt and diamond rings, Louisa guessed that Mr. Moon was a movie producer or director.

As she passed Moon's seat, she glanced back. Both men were staring at her backside. Twist winked while Moon smiled broadly and puckered his lips.

The man at the window seat beside Moon quietly read the *Wall Street Journal.* The seat chart identified him as Mr. Perry.

Suddenly the young woman in seat A1 stood, facing Twist. To gain his attention, she touched his shoulder as if to say 'Don't ignore me.' Her face looked familiar to Louisa, an avid movie fan.

Louisa shook her head, wondering how she'd missed noticing the young woman's costume as she came aboard. The blonde wore a short black leather miniskirt with matching knee-high boots. If the leather ensemble didn't draw attention, the see-through hot pink blouse did.

Twist nodded at the touch and patted her hand.

Louisa referred to the seat chart showing the blonde's name was Gloria. Suddenly Louisa recognized her as the star of the last film she'd watched on HBO. Widely advertised as the next Marilyn, Gloria's last film was a box office success.

Wonder if she's angling for a new role under the wealthy Mr. Twist. Louisa grinned.

Gloria, smiling intently at Twist, blinked slate blue eyes while nodding toward the forward restroom.

Checking his watch, Twist stood and followed her into the small restroom.

Conversation interrupted, Moon leaned back in his seat as Gloria and Twist shut the restroom door behind them.

Unbelieving, Louisa caught her breath. She turned to study the reactions of the other first class passengers.

Balancing a tray of cheese puffs and a large martini for his boss, Robert awkwardly stood aside as Gloria and Twist edged by, ignoring him.

Babbs, whom Louisa guessed was Twist's personal secretary, reddened with anger as the couple entered the restroom. Miffed, she refused the cocktail offered by Robert.

At his window seat, Perry rolled his eyes, turning to another page in his newspaper.

The seventh member of the Twist party sat in seat B3, noting Louisa's reaction as well as those of his fellow travelers.

The man joked. "Wasn't it lucky the restroom was vacant?" On the seating chart, Louisa identified him as Mr. Oliver.

"Otherwise, we'd have to witness them writhing in the aisle," he leaned forward, still watching Louisa.

He grinned at Louisa. "Might make a better movie than the ones I usually review." Then he added, "Or the so-called political blockbuster he's working on now."

Louisa shrugged. "If Mr. Twist is this busy all the time, how does he find time to make movies?"

Just then she backed into the drink cart being pushed up the aisle by Ann and Janie.

"No need for you two clowns going into first class today," she smirked, wondering if they had spotted Gloria and Twist enter the restroom together.

"Their drinks are being taken care of by that person," she nodded toward Robert, busily serving the five travelers still seated in first class.

THREE

Irritated at Louisa's comment, Ann and Janie began returning the jingling drink cart to the rear galley.

"Spotted that Mr. Perfect yet?" Ann asked Janie sotto voce as they moved into the economy plus and economy sections.

"Just maybe I have," Janie replied, stopping the cart beside aisle seat C8.

"I owe this gentleman another refreshment."

Janie beamed at the large man squeezing her hand while palming a bill. Wearing a loose tropical shirt, he appeared as expansive as his smile. Curling gray hair topped a bronzed Caribbean face. Brown eyes twinkled as Janie mixed him a second and stronger rum collins.

He regarded her with another dazzling grin. "I owe you my life."

At Janie's nod, Ann resumed pulling the cart to the rear. Once in the galley, she exhaled loudly. "Who is that gorgeous pirate?"

Janie opened her hand to show Ann the twenty-dollar bill and card she clutched.

"Jan Kokk, private investigator," she read aloud. Then with a giggle, "and an LA hotel telephone number."

Ann frowned, reaching for the card. "Better steer clear of that one," she advised.

"Can't you just imagine him with a black eye-patch and sword? He looks like a real life corsair. Besides that," she tilted Janie's chin. "He's too old for you, girl. But he's just right for me!"

Janie wrested the card back. "Forget it! You're not getting this."

"Whatever," Ann began dumping drink remains into a trash compartment.

"He's certainly perked up your morale," Ann blinked at Janie. "Minutes ago you were threatening our boss with bloody murder."

Janie paused while emptying the cart trash. "I still have it in for that old biddy.

"I'm mad about being called a look-alike for that TV program. What's its name, again?"

"*Hot in Cleveland.* You're supposed to resemble the short, younger girl called Melanie. I'm the skinny, tall Vicky character."

"Well…I don't appreciate that one bit! And I'm **not** from Cleveland! I'm from Shamrock, Texas!"

"Cool it, Janie. Don't make a fuss or you'll find yourself back in Shamrock sooner than you'd like."

--

Wishing she were wearing her contacts, Louisa stood in front of the curtain separating first class from the back of the airplane. She wanted to see the movie starlet and Twist, the designated star-maker, as they struggled out the small restroom.

How could they have possibly managed anything in that teeny closet-like space?

Ten minutes, tops, she predicted, glancing at her watch for the third time. Would the others in first class ignore the two? Maybe even applaud?

As if on cue, Twist came out of the restroom to return to his seat. Sans silk tie, he posed beside his B2 seat, grinning at the others.

His grin was erased by puzzlement as he glanced down at his seat cushion.

Twist scooped up an envelope on his seat, then sat. With a flourish, Robert prepared to spread a linen napkin in his boss's lap, preparatory to lunch.

To everyone's alarm, Twist stood suddenly, holding aloft the envelope. "What's this?" he demanded.

Twist's half-lidded eyes and red face obviated words. He shook the envelope in Robert's face.

"What's this?" he repeated.

Adding to the drama, the restroom door opened and blonde Gloria appeared. All talk, even Twist's, stopped.

Having taken the time to touch-up makeup and straighten her miniskirt and blouse, Gloria appeared normal, except for the look she gave Twist.

Threatening Robert with the mysterious envelope, Twist was oblivious to her endearing glance. Ignored, she sat down heavily in seat A1, crossed her legs and opened a flight magazine.

Frightened by Twist's anger, Robert blanched, miming ignorance of the envelope while retreating toward Louisa.

"Where'd that envelope come from?" Frozen-faced, Robert challenged Louisa in the same tone he'd just received.

"No idea," she shrugged. "Didn't notice it in his chair a minute ago. But I've been in the rear," she inclined her head toward the economy section.

Enjoying Robert's panic, she fractionally adjusted his bow tie. "Get with it, Sonny. Hadn't you better serve lunch now?"

FOUR

The previous Tuesday, Jan Kokk sat on his usual stool at his favorite beach bar in Willemstad, capital of Curacao. Languidly he stretched, toying with an icy bottle of Amstel beer, and watched the small inbound waves darken the white sands in front of him

Kokk prided himself in his reputation as Curacao's foremost private investigator. But lately business had been slow. Even the island's divorce cases, his least favorite, had dwindled.

Several personal bills were overdue. One was for the replacement of the smooth, no-tread tires on his small Citroen coupe. Another was the monthly bill for his favorite cognac.

"Thought I'd find you here, Jan."

Without turning, Kokk recognized the familiar voice behind him. It was his colleague and former classmate at the Police Academy who eventually became chief of police.

Chief Felix van Hooser sat on the adjoining stool with a thump, motioning to the bartender for a beer. He slid his visor-encrusted service hat toward Kokk.

"Haven't seen much of you since your return from Las Vegas, Jan," van Hooser placed his chief's baton on the bar.

"Always a pleasure seeing our famous chief of police," Kokk acknowledged. "Especially if he's buying the beer."

Van Hooser chuckled deeply. "That's just the start of the opportunity I'm offering you. How'd you like another posh, expenses-paid trip to the States?"

Kokk straightened on the stool, looking intensely at his friend. "Are you kidding? Salary? Expenses?"

Van Hooser sipped his beer. He grinned. *My fish is on the hook.*

"Yes, I expect so, Jan. But oddly the funds aren't from my miniscule police budget."

"Then where?"

"Our foreign ministry."

Van Hooser grinned at Kokk's expression. "Since I knew you'd be eager, I already made you an appointment to discuss this possible assignment with the ministry executive. Will tomorrow at ten do you?"

Van Hooser slid off his stool. Standing, he drained his beer. "My friend's paying," he waved to the bartender.

"Wear a tie and a clean shirt, Jan. And don't be late."

--

The next afternoon Kokk stood outside the office door of the chief of police, chatting with van Hooser's new secretary and pulling off the necktie he'd dutifully worn all morning.

He eyed the attractive young woman. "You're a delightful change from old Edith. What happened to her?"

She replaced the telephone with which she'd just announced Kokk's arrival. "Retired, Mr. Kokk. You can go right in."

"We should celebrate your new job," he paused beside her desk, "with dinner tonight. I'll come here for you at closing?"

Once inside van Hooser's spacious, high ceiling office, he was motioned to a chair next to the chief's massive desk. "How'd it go, Jan? Get the job?"

Kokk reached over the desk to shake van Hooser's hand. "Thanks to your recommendation, Felix. Yes, I was accepted for this peculiar assignment."

"Tell me about it."

Kokk cleared his throat. "It's confidential, as I'm sure you know."

"Yes. I know the problem but not the details."

"Our minister plenipotentiary, also known as Curacao's consul at Los Angeles, is sinking in serious debt over there. My job is to return him to Curacao to face the minister's scrutiny and scolding. Forcibly return him if necessary.

"Most importantly, I must keep him quiet and away from the press. We don't want his indiscretions publicly known."

Van Hooser hitched his big chair closer. "Forcibly means you're authorized to arrest him in the US?"

"Yes but only as a last resort. That's why I'm to ask you to issue me cuffs and a firearm for the trip.

"Oh," Kokk added. "And documents allowing me to carry a sidearm on the airplane and in the US."

"When's your flight?"

"Leaving Hato airport at nine in the morning, so I can catch a noon departure from Miami to LA."

Van Hooser nodded, reaching down to extract a bundle from a desk drawer. "Sign the receipt and it's all yours until your happy return with our indiscreet diplomat."

Kokk unwrapped the bundle and examined its contents: a holstered police short-barrel revolver, a box of ammunition, handcuffs and keys. He signed the receipt the chief edged toward him.

"I'm obliged to you, Felix."

"I know you'll do us proud, Jan. Quietly proud, without headlines," he emphasized. "Anything else?"

"Can't get my car back until I pay the repair bill. Can someone give me a lift to Hato airport early tomorrow morning?"

Grinning, van Hooser rose to again shake his friend's big hand. "I plan on picking you up myself at eight.

"But try to send my new secretary home before then."

FIVE

Twist tore open and read the note in the mysterious envelope found in his vacant seat. Still standing, he glared accusingly at each member of his party.

"Who did this?" he demanded.

No one replied, adding to his rage.

"Who put this in my chair?

"Change seats with me, Oliver," he commanded. "I don't want anyone seated behind me!"

Hurriedly, Oliver moved into Twist's former chair in the second row. Twist sat down in Oliver's just-vacated seat and motioned to the wide-eyed Robert.

"I need a drink." Twist declared, eyes still smoldering. "And be quick.

"No, don't go away," he added. "I want to see you mix it right here in front of me."

Robert retrieved a vodka bottle from the drink cart and poured a hefty shot over ice. He handed it to Twist.

Twist looked at the drink suspiciously. "Now **you** drink it!"

Forehead glistening, Robert gulped the drink he'd just prepared for his boss. He stood, holding the empty glass, awaiting further orders from the irascible Roger Twist.

"Now fix me another one just like it."

This time Twist accepted the glass and tasted it experimentally.

"I'm skipping lunch," he announced. "You may serve the others."

He held up a staying hand. "But first ask all the attendants who put that damned envelope in my seat."

--

Moon was the first of the Twist party to muster enough nerve to move to row 3 and sit beside Twist, his old friend and associate.

Moon began quietly, earnestly. "I know something's wrong, Roger. What is it?" He whispered, "Maybe I can help?"

Warily, Twist looked sideways at the director and producer with whom he'd collaborated since his initial film success years ago. That instantly popular movie was called *The Seventh Wife.*

The Broadway version had flopped but Moon and his writer-wife convinced aspiring newcomer Twist that the play still had promise. All it needed was their concentrated, 24/7 effort.

The three secluded themselves in Moon's Lake Placid retreat. After three months of rewrite/critique/rewrite, a new script emerged like the legendary phoenix.

Critics so acclaimed the new *Seventh Wife* film that its success was immediate. Almost lost in Twist's and Moon's hysteria of sudden fame was the drowning death of Moon's wife in a boating accident. The details of her death--during a weekend of sailing and celebratory boozing --never were made public.

Moon motioned to Robert. "Scotch on the rocks, Robert. Better make it a double."

Emboldened by the drink, Moon tried again. "What's wrong, Roger? Tell me. How can I help?"

Twist finished his drink and handed the empty to Robert. After a refill, he motioned Robert away.

Twist studied his seatmate. "Not sure I can trust you or anyone else on this plane, old friend. But here goes."

He took a deep breath and lowered his voice. "I've received a death threat!"

Moon looked incredulous. "You? Threatened? Who did it? You mean…in Brazil?"

"No, right here." Twist waved his free hand. "Right here on this damn airplane!"

"What were the words? How exactly were you threatened?"

Angrily, Twist knocked his drink askew. "Wrong tense! I **am** in danger here and now! Don't you get it?

"I need protection or I may not reach LAX!"

Frantically, Moon waved at Louisa seated in a fold-down near the front door. "Yes sir?" she responded.

Moon leaned forward to speak in her ear. "Do you know if there's a US marshal on this flight? Or a law enforcement officer of any kind?

"We need immediate help!"

SIX

He was slowly transcribing an email to van Hooser in Curacao. It was slow going due to the size of Kokk's fingers and the tablet's tiny keypad.

"Mr. Kokk? Mr. Jan Kokk?"

A well-dressed older man stood in the aisle beside Kokk's C8 seat.

"Yes?" Kokk looked up, frowning at the interruption. Now he'd have to begin the email all over.

"Mr. Kokk, my name is Harold Moon and I'm an associate of Mr. Roger Twist. Perhaps you've heard of Roger? He's a famous movie executive."

"Afraid not, Mr. Moon." Although excellent with names Kokk never had heard of this one.

Kokk sighed. "How may I help you?"

"Mr. Twist and I would be delighted if you'd join us up forward for a drink or two and a confidential word."

Having placed the tablet in the seat pocket ahead of him, Kokk happily rose and stretched. "I'm both delighted and curious.

"Besides, my patience is becoming as thin as this tiny seat cushion."

In the first class section, Oliver, the movie critic, moved to the vacant second row seat. The third row was vacant except Twist had moved into the starboard window chair.

"Mr. Twist, Mr. Kokk."

Kokk studied the graying, well-tailored Roger Twist, noting his expensive shirt, links and gold Rolex. An expensive Italian silk tie would have completed the picture of easy wealth.

Kokk accepted the seat next to Twist. Moon sat on the aisle.

"Thank you for coming, Mr. Kokk," Twist emitted a gasp, making Kokk wonder if illness was the next topic.

"I apologize for the hasty summons, but…"

Twist stopped in the midst of the welcome, looking intently at Kokk. "I'm told you are armed, Mr. Kokk?"

Kokk nodded, uncomfortable with this turn of conversation. "How did…"

Twist interrupted, grinning broadly. "The plane's manifest, Mr. Kokk. The FAA requires it to identify any passenger authorized to carry a firearm. Once we explained my dilemma, the flight attendant shared your identity with us.

"I'm forgetting myself," Twist raised his voice. "Drinks, Robert! What will you have, Mr. Kokk? Have you had lunch? If not, Robert can prepare you a…"

It was Kokk's time to interrupt. "I'm fine, thanks. But a hearty rum collins would be most welcome."

After drinks arrived and Robert shooed away, Twist began a monologue. From his aisle seat, Moon leaned forward, nodding encouragement.

"I'm returning from the Brazilian film festival with an idea--the genesis--for an epic motion picture I feel I must make. All I have at the moment is an incomplete script that I obtained in Sao Paulo from a reliable source.

"I just received this envelope," he took it from his vest, "on the plane just a few minutes ago from an unknown person who placed it in my chair while I was…elsewhere."

Moon couldn't resist a grin, knowing that 'elsewhere' meant closeted in the restroom with an ambitious starlet.

"The note herein," Twist shook the envelope theatrically, "threatens my life unless I abandon my intended project **before** we reach LA."

Kokk sat back, musing. "You don't think it could be a hoax?"

Moon interjected, "We can't take that chance, Mr. Kokk. Unfortunately, we have serious enemies in the entertainment business. They'd enjoy eliminating a competitor like Mr. Twist."

Twist agreed. "Especially a competitor who can produce my kind of enlightened entertainment. That's why our conversation must be treated confidentially, Mr. Kokk."

"Of course," Kokk sipped the collins. "But why are you sharing this with me? I'm not a bodyguard.

"I'm on an official assignment for the government of Curacao. I cannot imagine how I might resolve your, uh, dilemma."

"Expert advice doesn't come cheaply, Mr. Kokk," Moon rolled his eyes.

Kokk set his unfinished drink on a tray. "Being employed by you for security advice while working for Curacao would be highly unethical, if not criminal.

"I thank you for the drink, Mr. Twist," Kokk arose stiffly, preparing to return to his seat in the economy plus section. "An intriguing problem. Hopefully it's merely a hoax or trick being played on you."

"Please sit down, Mr. Kokk. I must apologize for my abruptness. I'm not used to coaxing.

"Another libation for Mr. Kokk, Robert!" Twist called.

"Please allow me five more minutes of your time," Twist pleaded.

"First I genuinely feel that my life is jeopardized on this aircraft. If I don't renounce this once-in-a-lifetime opportunity to produce an impelling, important mega-documentary, I may not reach California alive.

"All I ask of you, sir, is your presence here beside me. In my opinion, you are my life insurance. Please just sit here, keeping me company.

"Is that too much to ask of another human being?"

Moon wiped his eyes with an initialed handkerchief. "Please help us, Mr. Kokk," he added to Twist's plea.

Kokk sat silently, studying Roger Twist.

Robert placed a fresh drink on Kokk's tray.

Finally, Kokk nodded. "I'd be inhuman not to assist you. Were you to die as a result, I'd be dismayed."

Kokk pointed at the fresh drink. "Robert, take it away, please.

"Then I'll stay."

SEVEN

When Moon excused himself to use the restroom, Kokk turned to Twist. "I need to know as much as possible about this new project which, you feel, jeopardizes your life.

"Then I'd like you to review these people for me," Kokk waved his hand at the others in first class. "I need to know about their disputes, anger, animosities…anything you can tell me.

"But first, show me that threatening note you found in your chair."

"Here," Twist offered the note. "I suppose any fingerprints are blurred if that's what you're after."

It was written on plain paper, common to computer printers. In awkward, all capital, child-like print, the message said:

> UNLESS YOU IRREVOCABLY AND
> PERMANENTLY HALT
> THE PROJECT BASED ON THE DIARY YOU STOLE,
> YOU WILL NOT REACH LOS ANGELES ALIVE.
> TO LIVE, YOU MUST IMMEDIATELY
> PUBLICLY ANNOUNCE THE
> FOLLOWING: EFFECTIVE NOW, I
> IMMEDIATELY CANCEL ALL PLANS TO
> PUBLICIZE IN ANY MANNER ANY
> INFORMATION CONCERNING THE LATE
> BELOVED VENEZUELAN PRESIDENT.
> ROBERT G. TWIST.

"Recognize the style of writing?" Kokk probed. "Any of the words remind you of someone? Or the awkward printing?"

Twist shook his head. "Looks like the crazy who wrote it used his or her off hand."

Kokk glanced at Twist, remembering a first impression that the multimillionaire was ill. "Are you taking any medication?"

Twist appeared deflated, exhausted by nerves or worry about the next few hours which might be his last. "Only a little yellow capsule for my heart. It's digitoxin.

"I hid a couple of them in the restroom while I was in there with Gloria. Just in case I needed them in an emergency."

He pounded his chest. "Sound as a Swiss franc," he boasted. "I didn't miss a beat with Gloria when I--ah, interviewed--her just now."

As Moon returned, Kokk arose and spoke to him briefly. Assenting, Moon reoccupied his initial seat in the second row, forward of where Kokk and Twist huddled.

"Another drink might help," Twist signaled Robert.

Kokk shook his head. "I'd prefer that you didn't." With that, Kokk waved Robert back to his chair in the front row.

"No alcohol. This is a time for you to be clear-headed while I pick your brain," Kokk began. "Let's start with the obvious. Who do you think wants to kill you?"

Denied a drink, Twist frowned. "I don't trust any of those characters seated there," he waved at the front two rows.

"I've had serious problems with all of them. Were you to put it to a secret ballot, each one would vote me dead. They're well paid hangers-on."

Animated, Twist waved his hand in the air. "Their absurd salaries keep them here, not loyalty or devotion to me. I'm generous-to-a-fault, good ole Roger Twist."

Derisively, Twist appraised his colleagues who were avidly watching *Guardians of the Galaxy,* the first class section's thriller movie.

"What does their rapt attention say about today's quality of available movie entertainment?

"Shocking!" he answered himself. "And look at my esteemed film critic sitting there, enjoying that adolescent film."

"Who?"

"Oliver there," Twist pointed at the critic's back. "He's laughing, even taking notes for his next high-priced review.

"He'd better not pan my coming production. It'll rival *The Ten Commandments!*

"In the past he's acted the spoiler for several of my early films. He'd better not try that again!"

Kokk stood up to remove his one and only suit coat. Carefully he hung it on the aisle seat across from him. "So you're not canceling your project? You're ignoring the death threat?"

"Damn right!" Twist chuckled. "With you here beside me, I feel invincible! Maybe you're right. It could be just a hoax, a malicious trick played on me by one of my many detractors."

Twist pointed to the six people sitting ahead of him. "Maybe it's one of them sitting right there, enjoying my food, drink and generous salary!

"God, I'm parched," he exclaimed. "How about that drink now?"

EIGHT

Kokk held out his hand to halt a passing attendant. It was Janie, the one he'd earlier handed his card.

She blinked long eyelashes in anticipation. "Yes, Mr. Kokk?"

"Could you bring me a bottle of cold water, unopened?"

"Certainly. That's easy," she tittered. "How about I hang up your coat, too? Are you going to stay up here instead of in the back with me?"

"I hope you might continue serving me. I'm up here with a friend."

"Consider it done." She marched to the forward galley for the water. "Here you are, sir."

"Thank you, Janie. I hope I'm not getting you in Dutch--a phrase I hate--with your supervisor?"

She beamed. "Just call for Janie and I'll be here."

She trounced to the rear, knowing Kokk's amused eyes followed her.

Kokk twisted open the bottle of water and handed it to Twist.

"Thanks, Mr. Kokk. I appreciate the water plus your little maneuver to get us served separately from the front. Which leads me back to the subject of compensation."

Kokk shook his head. "As I said, I can't accept any compensation since I'm performing an official service for my government.

"Instead," Kokk turned on his overhead reading light, "please tell me as much as you will about this new project which endangers you."

Twist carefully wiped his lips with a napkin. "It's amazing! That's not a word Roger Twist uses often, Mr. Kokk."

"Jan."

"Fine, Jan. I'm Roger."

"So I'm in Sao Paulo, being besieged by several very attractive young women, all seeking contact or contract or both, of course.

"One night I was approached by one of them who claimed she had been the mistress of the late dictator of one of the Latin nations. She claimed to have somehow 'acquired' his personal diary which she offered to sell to me.

"As you know from reading that threat I received a few hours ago, that dictator was the president of Venezuela."

22

Kokk nodded.

"Can you imagine? I have access to his personal account about the growth of each of the radical political movements, which assisted--no--thrust** him forward.

"From something called the Fifth Republic movement to another political body named the Bolivian Revolution, finally to the United Socialist Party of which he became *El Supremo.*

"Each movement provided a stepping stone to his ultimate power, meaning presidency of an entire nation. Why, his personal diary's a South American version of *Mein Kampf!*

"What a treasure! No one in Hollywood, Europe or South America has my abilities to weave his narrative into an epic motion picture.

"Me, Roger Twist." Panting, he tapped his chest. "This film will be my lasting legacy. I'll be as well known as Sam Goldwyn."

Exhausted from his effort, Twist slid back into the depths of his chair.

"No, Jan. I won't give it up. No, sir! Would you?"

Rather than answer, Kokk theorized. "Perhaps this threat against your life doesn't originate from the six people sitting ahead of us but from foreign governments not wanting their comrade's life publicized? Cuba, Venezuela, Bolivia and Nicaragua come to mind."

"Possibly," Twist acknowledged. "But anyone of those six," he pointed at his group, "could be the paid agent of those countries.

"All of them," again he swept his hand over the front two rows, "would delight in my demise.

"But we're going to beat them! Keep me safe, Jan Kokk." With that Twist closed his eyes and fell asleep.

NINE

As Janie sauntered down the aisle, Ann made a face. "I saw you conniving up there in first class. Who charmed you this time? Was it the Mr. Perfect I predicted you'd meet back here in economy?"

Janie grinned. "My secret, girl friend. Now I'm on call to serve someone up there, too."

"Who?"

"You remember the guy you called a gorgeous pirate?"

"The one seated…" she stopped. "Oh, I see! He moved up front."

Arms akimbo, Ann confronted her friend. "Really, Janie! He's too old for you. And a foreigner?"

Janie again flouted the card Kokk gave her. He had added the name of his LA hotel. She flicked Ann's chin with the card then quickly pocketed it.

"You'll never talk me out of this card, Annie Fannie."

"Harrumph," Ann said in disgust. "And just what are you planning on doing with it?"

Janie parodied a yawn. "I think a layover in LA would do wonders for my fatigued state."

"Ha! Louisa will never allow you to layover, not after you smarted off to her about not being from Cleveland."

"I'm certainly **not** anything like that female from that TV show, either," Janie grimaced.

--

In the cockpit of the 737, Captain Bringuel sat at the controls, enjoying the musical antics of First Officer Benson sitting beside him.

Benson took off his headset. "Houston control just handed us off to San Antonio, Skipper."

"Well, since you're from Taxas," Bringuel exaggerated an accent. "Let's hear another little song."

Beaming, Benson reached behind his chair and retrieved a worn Stetson cowboy hat. He put it on with a whoop. "Yah-hoo! How about *San Antonio Rose,* potnah? Know it?"

Parodying Benson, Bringuel cried "Let 'er rip, potnah!"

In a raspy voice, Benson began,

> **"Deep within my heart**
> **Lies a melody**
> **A song of old San Antone..."**

Now Benson pretended to play a guitar while imitating a yodel.

> **"Moon in all your spendor..."**

Louisa, the chief attendant, managed to unlock the cockpit door while holding aloft a coffee tray. Hearing the two males loudly singing off-key, she slammed shut the door to prevent the passengers from hearing.

> **"Rose, my rose of San Antone..."**

Bringuel and Benson increased their singing an octave to celebrate Louisa's arrival with fresh coffee.

> **"Like petals falling apart..."**

"C'mon, Louisa! Sing!"

"Don't know the words," she alibied. Their singing stopped abruptly as she handed out the steaming coffee.

"You two sounded mighty pretty," she fibbed. "I hope the cabin speakers weren't on."

Benson laughed. "I bet most of our passengers back there know the song. They could all join in and we'd be in LA before you can say 'Howdy, potnah! Gitty-up!'"

Bringuel broke the spell. "How are our passengers doing back there?"

"No complaints so far, sir. Of course, they're all asking if we'll make LAX on time. They want to have someone waiting for them at the terminal."

"How about our first class toadies? I heard you call the boss toad 'Mister Big.'"

"Something's going on with Mr. Big. I'm not sure what. He's called forward that big passenger from economy who's authorized to carry a weapon. The two of them are in deep conversation about something."

Bringuel looked perturbed as Benson answered Louisa's question. "We should be on time. But currents over the Hill Country can be volatile this time of year. It could get bumpy before long. Better alert our dazzling flight attendants to tighten their cinches."

"And keep us informed of what's happening with Mr. Big and his armed friend." Bringuel made a face as Louisa left the cockpit with their empty cups.

TEN

As the movie in first class ended, five passengers huddled around Moon. "What's going on with Roger?"

"Who's the big fellow he's talking to back there in the third row?"

"Why did you suddenly change seats? Did Roger tell you to move?"

Unwilling to share everything, Moon hesitated. "The boss is perturbed about a perceived problem. That big man sitting with him is apparently advising about the problem…if there is one."

"What kind of problem?" Perry, the attorney and tax advisor leaned forward.

"Let's just say that Roger is **edgy** until we get home."

Gloria spoke up, checking her lipstick in a small mirror. "Bet I can calm him down."

Twist's personal secretary, Babbs, rolled her eyes in derision. "I think we've already seen your best efforts at 'calming' as you call it. Apparently, you failed."

"Lady, I don't know what failure is," Gloria glared. "But I bet you do!"

Oliver, the movie critic, held up a hand to stop the tirade. Then he punched Robert's shoulder. "How about feeding us? I'm famished after that movie."

"Yeah." Perry joined in. "How about it, Robert? I could do with a big drink, too."

Unhappy that Kokk was receiving all his boss's attention, Robert scowled.

An alternative made him brighten. "Sure. I'll ask the chief attendant to serve us."

--

"Tell me about your friends," Kokk waved at the six people accompanying Twist.

"Friends? Your choice of the word is curious, Jan. One of them must have written that hate note and wants me dead. Dead before we even make LA.

"Call that a friend?

"Among them must be the crazy who wants me dead before we land."

Kokk touched Twist's shoulder to stop the monologue. "Tell me about each of them. Maybe we can ferret out the guilty one. Perhaps there's more than one attempting to frighten you."

Mollified, Twist sat up, staring at the others.

"That one's Gloria, in seat A1, who keeps winking at me. Sure, she's a blonde knockout, even has some talent.

"But one of her earlier films, *Vegas Model,* bombed. Now she's offering me anything and everything for a major part in my planned production.

"I'm considering her to play the dictator's mistress. She already knows the part," Twist tittered. "I personally coached her just an hour ago."

"Sounds like Gloria has good reason to prefer you alive and signing checks rather than dead." Kokk made notes in a small notebook. "What about that other lady in the front row?"

"Oh, that's old Babbs, my personal secretary for twelve--maybe thirteen--years. Takes care of my schedules, interviews, meetings, prescriptions, credit cards. Things like that."

"Why do you mistrust her if she's taken care of your expenses and all that for many years?"

"I have good reasons not to trust her." Wishing for a cigarette, Twist drummed fingers on his empty drink tray.

"I discovered she shared info about Twist Enterprises with another studio a couple of years ago. Her favorite cousin was the go-between. I immediately canned him.

"Babbs, the old bat, has never forgiven me for that. Hell, I'd do it again!"

"Moon?"

"Never trusted him. Years ago, when we were reworking *The Seventh Wife,* his wife drowned in a boating accident. Although Moon never accused me, he's always blamed me for her death.

"She and I were close."

Twist held up an index finger crossed with the middle digit. "This close," he leered.

Kokk snorted. "Who's the man in seat F1, next to Robert?"

"That's Perry, my tax expert. He's been a brick so far but only because he knows I've got my eye on him. Back in the 50's he ran a tax scam shop in Westwood.

"If I were out of the way, he'd run wild again. Probably he'd write a tell-all about my tax shenanigans, too. He'd make a million in royalties!"

"The man seated in your former seat?"

"That's Oliver, always hungry Oliver. He's valuable to me in dual roles. He's not only a well-respected movie critic but a competent background writer as well.

"I'm depending on his favorable reviews of my planned movie to boost it like a moon shot. I've decided to call the movie *Life of a Dictator.*

He nudged Kokk. "What do you think of the title? Or maybe *Democratic Dictator?*"

Kokk blinked. "*Death of a Dictator* sounds more macabre. I thought *noir* was a favorite Hollywood theme nowadays.

"Back to your six 'associates.' Is that a better description of them? We're left with Robert, your majordomo."

"He'd love you for that description," Twist chortled. "I mean that literally."

Kokk's pen paused over the notebook. "You trust him?"

"Only because he knows I can blacklist him anytime I take a notion. Without my reference--and a damn good one--he'd never find a job as cushy as this."

Kokk snapped shut his notes. "Like glamorous Gloria, Robert sounds like someone who wants you alive and well. He depends on you for his livelihood."

"They all appear that way, Jan," Twist waved despondently toward the six. "You know what we say in the movies? Appearances can lie."

ELEVEN

"How about a real drink now?"

"Not yet, Roger." Kokk wagged a hand at Janie standing in the back of the plane.

"Instead, how about something to eat from the economy galley? Are you hungry?"

"Sure. That shrimp salad was a snack rather than a meal."

Appearing at Kokk's side wearing fresh lip-gloss and moisturizer, Janie bent to his eye level. "How may I help, Mr. Kokk?"

He looked into her eyes. "Call me Jan, for starters. Think Mr. Twist and I could be served dinner from your galley just as if we were seated with you?"

In minutes she wheeled up two dinners despite frowns from Louisa standing like a sentinel in first class.

"Here you are, gentlemen. Enjoy."

Kokk palmed a bill into a spare napkin and returned it to her. "I hope you and I might share dinner at my hotel tonight."

Cocking her head, a smiling Janie trounced back to the rear, ignoring another bout of frowns from Louisa.

Before they had finished the chicken alfredo, Janie was back. This time she was disheveled and distressed, not at all the alluring poised female who had just served their dinners.

She looked ashen as she touched Kokk's arm. "Please, Mr. Kokk.

"Please. Come with me right now."

"What's wrong?"

"Someone has written a threat on one of the back restroom mirrors. Ann just found it.

"We're scared silly! We don't know what to do about it other than alert the captain. Can you come and help--uh, advise--us, please?" she wailed.

Kokk unbuckled his belt and arose, beckoning to Twist. "I expected something like this," he conceded.

"Get up, Roger. Stay with me. I don't want you out of my sight!"

The two men followed Janie to the rearmost restroom where a shaking Ann waited beside the open door.

On the restroom mirror was a lipstick scrawl:

A BOMB IN YOUR BAGGAGE HOLD
WILL EXPLODE AT 7:15 PM LOCAL

Twist gasped and grabbed his chest as he mumbled the message aloud. Kokk guided him into the chair vacated by Ann. "Take deep breaths," he instructed the red-faced multimillionaire. "You're going to be okay."

With his cell phone, Kokk photographed the message, then lifted Twist back to his feet.

"C'mon," he motioned for Janie to precede him. "We're all going forward to see your captain. You come, too, Roger. I'm not leaving you behind."

To Ann, Kokk directed, "Lock the door. Keep everyone out. It's a crime scene now."

"Hurry," he urged Janie. "It's already 6:56 according to my pocket watch."

Looking alarmed at their approach, Louisa stood in front of the cockpit door, barring the way.

"You can't go in there."

"Janie just discovered a bomb threat. Open up! We need to tell the captain **now.**"

Louisa's aghast look riled Kokk. "Two decisions," he growled.

"The first is yours to unlock this door. The second is your captain's--to decide where to land immediately.

"Don't deny him enough time to react.

"Open that door!"

With that Louisa fumbled with the door combination and Kokk opened it. He pushed Janie in first, then turned to Louisa.

"Keep an eye on Mr. Twist for me. Don't let anyone near him! Make him sit down! Try to calm him."

--

Both pilots looked alarmed at the invasion of their sanctum. First Officer Benson began to unbuckle his seat harness.

"You can't come in…" he started.

Shoving him back into his chair, Kokk held out the cell phone to Captain Bringuel.

"This astute young lady found this message written on a mirror in a back lavatory. Read it, Captain.

"Then make a decision. The lives of your passengers and crew may depend on your reaction."

Wincing, Captain Bringuel studied the threat in the cell phone photo, then glanced at his watch. He handed the cell phone to Benson.

"I'm declaring an emergency. You search for the nearest place we can land. We only have minutes to get her down safely and evacuate everyone.

"It's either a hoax or there's a maniac aboard with a death wish. I can't take the chance that the bomb isn't for real.

"What do you think, Mr.…."

Janie spoke first. "Kokk," she said. "Mr. Jan Kokk."

"You're doing splendidly, Captain," Kokk offered. "As we say in Dutch, *beter vormen veilig* than *jamer vinen*.

"Better safe than sorry."

--

While Captain Bringuel reported their danger to San Antonio and prepared for an emergency landing, First Officer Benson searched for the nearest airport in the Texas Hill Country below them.

"Got one, Skipper!" he exclaimed. "It's small but it is dead ahead of us. A small airport at Kerrville."

"We're descending, San Antonio Control, for emergency landing at Kerrville." Bringuel repeated, "Kerrville."

"Only two runways," Benson read aloud from his scanner. "Longest is 1850 meters."

"That'll have to do."

Bringuel began another transmission. "Kerrville Airfield, this is Southwest 236 declaring an emergency. Request immediate landing instructions. Over.

"Kerrville Airfield," he repeated the call, then sighed with relief when he received an answer.

--

Once outside the cockpit door, questions from Kokk and Louisa sharply collided.

"Where's Twist?"

"What's happening?"

"Janie will fill you in," Kokk patted her on the shoulder. "Where's Twist?" he repeated.

"He's in the restroom there," Louisa pointed. "Said he had to take a pill."

Interrupting her reply, Kokk knocked on the door of the first class restroom. "Roger? Are you all right?"

Like Captain Bringuel, Kokk repeated his message.

There still was no response from inside.

"Open the restroom door for me," he ordered Louisa. "Your passenger may be ill or passed out from the excitement."

Fumbling with a key, white-faced Louisa opened the door on her second try.

Before entering the restroom, Kokk eyed Janie. "Tell her what the captain decided.

"I think **you,**" he emphasized the word for Louisa's benefit, "should announce to the passengers to take their seats, fasten belts and prepare for an emergency landing."

He grinned at Janie before ducking into the restroom where Twist sprawled in the corner.

Janie plucked the microphone from Louisa's hand and began:

"Ladies and gentlemen, please resume your seats immediately and fasten your seat belts. Please return your tray tables to the upright position.

"Pass all loose material like drink cups to the attendant in the aisle."

She took a deep breath, wondering if Louisa would grab the microphone. "The captain is preparing to make a safe but emergency descent to land at a nearby airport.

"Like our captain, we must also make preparations for such a landing. When instructed to do so, place your head down, between your legs, covered with your pillow or blanket. Parents firmly fasten your children in their seats or hold them securely in your lap."

Janie waved down the hands sprouting in the air like wildflowers. "Due to this emergency, please hold all questions until we are safely on the ground.

"Follow my instructions and we'll all be safe. Questions later, after we've landed."

Frowning, Kokk emerged from the restroom.

"Lock it back," he told a dazed Louisa now taking her microphone from Janie.

He held out his palm. "And give me the key."

"But where's Mr. Twist?"

Kokk wiped his forehead and pointed. "He's in there.

"*Hemel!* He's dead!"

TWELVE

Feet on the console, Jane Spellman kept time to an old Willie Nelson tune.

"Mama, don't let your baby grow up to be a cowboy..." she repeated the plaintive lyrics.

FM 93.3, The Ranch, played softly in the background as she neared the end of her solo duty in the manager's combination office and tower of the Kerrville-Kerr County Airport.

Suddenly her reverie was broken by a strong transmission over the speaker. Scrambling, she reached for the logbook and began writing:

> "1702 hr:
>
> Rec'd incm from SW Flt 236, declaring an emergency.
>
> Requesting immed landing instructions."

> *Oh My God, am I dreaming? Is this a FAA exercise? Did some weasel set me up?"*

Taking deep breaths, Jane reassured herself. I can do this. Just follow the instructions in the manual.

She flipped pages until finding the one marked in red FOR EMERGENCY USE ONLY.

Rereading the words spoken by the captain of Flight 236, Jane highlighted her notes:

"Bomb to explode at 7:15 local

Emergency equipment to stand by

Evacuate passengers from the aircraft to the runway by chutes

Anticipate passenger injuries

Request landing instructions to include surface winds/turbulence."

She took a deep breath, then gave the Boeing 737 captain the current wind direction and velocity as well as repeating the number of the runway which she had just illuminated.

Jane knocked over her coffee as she quickly switched chairs from the radio to the telephone to alert local agencies.

First, she dialed the Kerrville Fire Department, asking for emergency assistance at the airfield for a distressed commercial aircraft.

Next she called the Sheriff's Department and asked the duty clerk to alert the entire department and the Explosive Ordnance Disposal (EOD) squad.

Peterson Regional Medical Center was the next to be called. Jane's voice vibrated from excitement as she outlined the emergency, requesting ambulances and that all area urgent care facilities be alerted.

Numbed from her efforts, she studied the emergency instructions, making sure she'd called every agency on the list.

In despair, she cried out, "Who or what did I miss?" Just then the airport manager burst through the door.

Recovering herself, Jane began. "Here's where we stand, Chief."

By rote she repeated the transmission she'd received from the airplane, the instructions she'd given the pilot and the agencies she'd just alerted.

"Good job, Jane," Bob Mitchell patted her shoulder. "Guess I'd better get on the horn and call the FAA. How many passengers did you say?"

She checked her scribbled log. "The pilot reported one hundred fifty six pax and crew of eight."

"And he said the bomb will go off at 7:30?"

"No sir. Seven fifteen."

"Damn," he gulped as he looked at the wall clock. "It's almost seven!

"That pilot had better hurry and get wheels down, doors open and escape chutes deployed."

Another fear sharpened his tone. "We're going to need buses, too, to carry the passengers to safety once they're down."

"I already called the bus company, sir. They're sending us four buses and a big van."

Mitchell voiced another fear. "My God! What if we have to keep them here overnight waiting for a replacement plane and crew? You'd better call a hotel or two to see who can accommodate all those people.

36

"And what about traffic management? Highway 27 out front will be a madhouse in a few minutes."

"Did I say 'good' job before?" Mitchell looked over at her as he cradled a telephone with his shoulder.

"I meant **great** job!"

THIRTEEN

Texas Highway 27 snakes out the southeast door of Kerrville, past the seven-story, red brick VA Medical Center, to the Kerrville-Kerr County Airport. The two lanes of Highway 27 become four in places to accommodate the going-to-work, returning-home traffic of commuters living in Center Point and Comfort to the east of the airport.

By seven o'clock, Highway 27 was filled with racing fire trucks, sheriff vehicles, highway patrol cars, ambulances, and buses, most with sirens screeching and red lights flashing.

City police joined in, separating emergency vehicles from the vehicles of rubber-neckers wondering what all the ruckus was about. The latter were motioned to halt on the sides of the highway.

Only a van from a local TV station was allowed to follow the official vehicles into the airport gate.

A TV weather reporter leaned out of the van door, attempting to describe the scene.

"There are enough vehicles, people and noise out here to rival a victory homecoming of Kerrville's Tivy High School football team." She cupped her lips to be heard over the din.

Wishing she'd combed her hair, she motioned the cameraman to sweep the crowds and vehicles. She maintained a determined monologue about the scene and what little was then known about the emergency causing this traffic crush on Texas 27.

Like tardy school children entering their classroom, the vehicular sirens and flashing lights went silent as the parade turned off the highway and into the airport gate.

Mooney Road led to the more remote areas of the airfield where Flight 236 rumbled across the tarmac behind a speeding jeep whose flashing rear sign urged "Follow Me."

Before the aircraft engines were stilled, escape chutes were deployed from each aircraft door. Looking like giant tendons, they were rapidly filled with passengers sliding down the chutes to the tarmac. Deputies directed the passengers to a safer area in the rear.

The aircraft captain and first officer were the first to be questioned by Sheriff Swartz, standing beside his command and communications vehicle. The aviators both pointed to Kokk and Janie just emerging from the escape chute.

"There they are, Sheriff. They reported the bomb threat to us."

Sheriff Swartz, over six feet tall and thin as a whip, typified the Texas peace officer. Dressed in a gray stockman's hat, levis, boots and holstered pistol, he stepped forward, pointing at Kokk.

"Bring him here" he ordered a deputy as he threw away the end of a well-chewed cigar.

--

The deputy pointed to the sheriff and Kokk limped over, followed by Janie.

The two big men studied each other for a moment. Kokk had never met a Texas lawman before and extended his big hand.

"Jan Kokk," he said, turning to Janie standing next to him. "And this is the alert young lady who reported the bomb threat written on a restroom mirror."

"Janie," Kokk began.

"Roland," she added her last name. "With Mr. Kokk's help, we immediately relayed the message to Captain Bringuel. It speeded his decision to land here."

"I'm Sheriff Swartz," he mumbled, looking at the manifest. "I see you are armed, Mr. Kokk. Why?"

Kokk dropped his ignored hand. "I'm a private investigator from Curacao on a confidential mission for my government.

"I'm empowered by my government to arrest a Curacao citizen-- forcibly, if necessary—-and return him home."

"Well," Swartz's granite eyes didn't waver. "You won't need your pistol while in Kerr County. Hand it over to the deputy here. You'll get it back when you leave."

Sheriff Swartz continued to stare at the big investigator. "Is it true there's a dead body on that aircraft?"

Kokk unhappily handed his pistol, butt first, to the deputy. "I want a receipt."

Returning to Swartz's question, Kokk responded. "Yes, Sheriff, it's true. A passenger, Mr. Roger Twist of Hollywood, expired in the forward rest room. I left his body locked in there to preserve the crime scene."

"Crime?" the sheriff scowled. "What crime?"

Kokk scowled back. "Possibly he died from a heart attack. I doubt it. Twist showed me a death threat he received on the airplane an hour or so before his death."

"We're not wild-west amateurs out here, Kokk. An autopsy will tell us if it was a heart attack or not."

The sheriff turned to his deputy. "Ask the explosive ordnance guys if they're ready to move in."

"An autopsy takes time, Mr...." the sheriff fumbled for a name.

"Kokk," Janie spoke up, taking her hand off Kokk's arm for the first time.

The sheriff glared at Kokk. "You don't expect me to hold a whole plane load of people as material witnesses pending completion of an autopsy?

"Besides, it probably **was** a heart attack."

Kokk demurred. "Mr. Twist genuinely feared for his safety on the airplane. He even tried to hire me as his bodyguard until we reached Los Angeles."

"Did you?"

"No, I told him I couldn't do that since I'm on an assignment for my government back in Curacao."

"Thanks for reminding me," Swartz leered. "I want your passport, too."

Eye to eye, the two studied each other.

Kokk broke the momentary silence. "You'll get my passport when I get your receipt for my pistol."

The sheriff held up a hand. "Deputy," he called. "Make out a receipt for that pistol and give it to this guy.

"Then escort him and the lady back to the van where we can formalize their statements."

At that moment the airport office began announcing the time over its speaker.

"Seven oh eight."

--

40

Law officers cordoned off a circle of approximately one-mile from the airplane to prevent anyone approaching closer.

The captain and first officer were the first to be interviewed by the sheriff and his investigators. Finished, they stood beside a sheriff-marked sedan, attempting to cell phone their airline's headquarters in Dallas.

Further behind the circle around the airplane milled the plane's unhappy passengers, being packed aboard buses and driven further from the plane for their safety.

Flight attendants walked the bus aisles, as they had on the airplane, trying to calm passengers. Some of their charges were dazed, several belligerent. All had questions.

"It's now 7:10, Sheriff," one of his deputies whispered.

"Roger that," Swartz replied. "Why are you whispering? In fifteen mikes, fifteen," he repeated, "tell the explosives team to approach the airplane and start looking for a bomb, if there is one."

FOURTEEN

The audience of firefighters, medical personnel, law officers and airport workers held collective breaths as the EOD team began walking toward the airplane.

Cautiously, the dozen members of the team, leading several explosive-sniffing dogs from Kerr and Kendall counties, approached the deserted Boeing 737.

"Seven fifteen," the airfield speaker blared as the captive audience listened, some smiling with relief, others unconvinced that the danger was over.

"No explosion!" Swartz excitedly waved his big hat in the air. He pounded Kokk's back. "It was a hoax! I told you!"

"Give it a few more minutes before we celebrate," Kokk warned. "Maybe the bomber's watch was off a few minutes. Better safe than sorry," Kokk repeated the phrase, this time in English.

The audience surrounding the aircraft barriers broke into cheers but were quickly silenced by the sheriff speaking on a bullhorn.

"Quiet! No yelling! The EOD team needs complete silence to do its work safely."

His angry gaze challenged the crowd. "Nobody approaches the plane until I give the all clear! Understand?"

"Seven twenty three," the speaker system in the control tower again blared the time. Many onlookers checked their watches and began breathing normally.

"Damn hoax," Sheriff Swartz repeated. "I knew it!"

"Let's hope so," Kokk nodded. "Otherwise we'd lose a corpse, two crime scenes as well as a several million dollar airplane."

"You're still using that word 'crime.'" Swartz handed back Kokk's Curacao investigator's license that he'd been studying.

"Once a medical doctor examines the body, I'm betting his opinion will be homicide, Sheriff."

Sheriff Swartz spit, while hearing the Explosive Ordnance Disposal team leader's report of all clear.

--

In the airport manager's office, Captain Bringuel and First Officer Benson sat drinking coffee while telephoning their headquarters for instructions.

"What'd they say?" Bob Mitchell wanted to know.

"They want us to service the plane, mount up and get to Los Angeles soonest. We're behind schedule already. You know how that kind of publicity hurts the company."

"Or any mention of a bomb scare," Benson added.

Bringuel warned against a quick departure. "They're also highly upset that a passenger has 'expired,'--their word--on our flight. They want to know all about that. We can't give them a quick answer."

"You'll have to ask the sheriff out there," Mitchell pointed to Swartz's command and control van near the aircraft.

"Until the FBI or the Texas Rangers arrive and take over, it's our sheriff's call."

Bringuel set aside his coffee. "That means we might have to overnight here?"

"Yep. So you'd better ask the company to fund lodging and meals for passengers and crew if we have to wait 'til morning."

"What's the name of this burg again?"

"Kerrville, Texas."

--

Kokk was the first to climb the rickety metal stairway to the airplane's rear door. Sheriff Swartz was close behind. The stairway trembled with their combined weight.

"I want you to see the lavatory where the threat message was written," Kokk said over his shoulder. "Janie, that young flight attendant, showed it to me."

Kokk handed him the keys to the two restrooms. "We've locked both for your crime scene team."

"What's this going to prove?" Swartz visualized himself at home, boots off, cold beer in hand, watching the Dallas Cowboys.

Kokk delayed, hoping the medical examiner could check Twist's body and form an initial opinion before he and the sheriff reached the forward restroom.

"I thought you'd want to see exactly what initiated our panic at 30,000 feet over Texas."

"Okay. Okay." Swartz shrugged his shoulders and motioned another of his deputies forward.

"Get our techs to check this mirror for fingerprints. And look everywhere for the lipstick used to write it."

Swartz leered. "Lipstick suggests a female wrote the hoax threat, agree?"

Kokk parried. "Could have been a male just as easily. "Those letters," he pointed at several on the mirror, "don't look feminine to me."

Checking his old-fashioned pocket watch, Kokk wished it were later. "Shall we see the other restroom up front, where the body is?"

Because of his size, Kokk slowly preceded Swartz through the economy and economy plus sections to the forward restroom. The door was open and the medical examiner stood outside, speaking into a transcriber. A photographer kneeling in the aisle snapped pictures of the body.

The county medical examiner, Doctor Harrell, nodded. "I'm just about done here, Sheriff. We're ready to remove the body."

Kokk introduced himself. "Any preliminary thoughts, Doctor?"

"I'll perform the autopsy first thing tomorrow. Takes time, you know."

The sheriff stared at the body. "Any contusions, Doc?"

"No?" Swartz said as Harrell shook his head. "Could have been a heart attack, I suppose?"

"Could have been," Harrell pursed his lips, used to early questions.

"Except there is a thin white residue on the lips," he admitted. "Plus a strong bitter odor."

"An alkaloid odor, Doctor?" Kokk pressed.

"I'll have my report ready for you in the morning, Sheriff."

Turning to Kokk, Harrell nodded. "Yep, the odor is unmistakable. I can't rule out alkaloid poisoning.

"Gentlemen, good evening." With that Doctor Harrell hurried down the staircase, followed by his team bearing the covered body of Roger Twist on a stretcher.

FIFTEEN

Neither the sheriff nor Kokk spoke until they were seated in the airport manager's office. Swartz stared belligerently at the big investigator from Curacao.

"This character," the sheriff began, nodding to Kokk in the next chair, "is a passenger and a private investigator." They sipped coffee with airport manager Mitchell and a just-arrived Texas Ranger captain named Hooks.

"He has no official standing in this case but claims to know the dead man, a Roger Twist of Hollywood. The deceased wanted to hire Kokk as a bodyguard during the flight.

"He believes that we may have a homicide here, somehow related to the bomb threat.

"That right, Mister Kokk?" Swartz emphasized the title.

"Correct, Sheriff." Kokk leaned back in his chair, turning to Captain Hooks, sitting next to him. Hooks had just assumed responsibility for the case.

"Someone on the plane left this death threat in Twist's chair." Kokk passed the letter to Hooks.

"Sometime later we found a scrawled bomb threat on a restroom mirror, resulting in the emergency landing here.

"During the ensuing panic, Twist entered another restroom, the one in the first class section.

"In my opinion he was poisoned somehow and died in that restroom."

Hooks tossed Kokk's passport and investigator's license that he'd been eyeing back on the table. "Motive?"

Kokk took a deep breath. "Mr. Twist was the host of the six passengers seated with him in first class. Apparently a wealthy filmmaker, he'd reserved the entire first class section for himself and his group."

"Relatives?" Hooks asked, looking up from jotting notes.

"No, they were either actual employees of Twist or shared business interests in his movie making."

Swartz glinted at Kokk. "Presuming you're right about Twist being a homicide, you think his killer is likely to be one or more of the six?"

"Yes, Sheriff." Kokk wished for his pipe left on the airplane. "I think that very likely."

"You see," Kokk regarded Hooks. "Twist told me that all six of these people would be happier were he gone."

"Gone?"

"Dead," Kokk clarified.

Hooks cleared his throat, looking at each of them across the table. "Since I'm the senior here until the Feds arrive to take over terror--maybe murder--investigations, I think we must overnight the passengers, crew and aircraft here."

Mitchell, the airport manager blanched. "Why not allow the flight to continue to LA and conduct the investigation from there?

"Since the bomb threat obviously was a hoax, the passengers are in no danger. Besides, our local facilities are rather limited. This is not a commercial airport, you know."

The sheriff agreed, thumping his big hat on the table. "Not only are our airport facilities limited, my department is already completely committed.

"Our hands are full. Two crime scenes, a bomb threat, a dead passenger, more than a hundred live ones to care for and an aircraft to guard!"

Swartz raised his big hands in a gesture. "We need help, Captain Hooks, just to analyze the two **possible** crime scenes on the airplane."

"Ranger help is on the way, Sheriff," Hooks assured him. "We'll investigate here and now while the evidence is relatively free from contamination.

"I intend to begin by unloading all the hold baggage and have your explosives experts check it to assure that absolutely no danger of an explosion exists."

Swartz sighed, lighting a cigar despite the no smoking signs posted in the office.

Almost in Hook's face, Mitchell frowned. "Must all passengers remain here or just those of possible interest mentioned by Mr. Kokk?"

Reaching for his cell phone, Captain Hooks arose.

"Everybody stays, gentlemen. Please pass the word.

"Now let's unload the hold baggage and have the explosives team check everything before allowing the passengers to reclaim their luggage."

SIXTEEN

Janie, Ann and the other attendants had their hands full while patrolling the bus aisles. Passenger questions and comments aboard the crowded buses parked on the edges of the field were unending and becoming more insistent.

> *Are we still in danger?*
> *Where's the restroom?*
> *I want the book I left on the airplane.*
> *Why are we cooped up on this bus?*
> *What's going on out there?*
> *What are those policemen doing?*
> *I want to smoke!*
> *Why can't we get back on the plane now?*

Louisa, the chief attendant, trotted from bus to bus, then back to the chief deputy for more information. "I feel like I've run the Boston marathon," she complained.

"How about you and your partner entertaining our passengers with something from *Hot in Cleveland*?" She poked Janie, pointing toward the unhappy passengers.

"I just bet you know several funny skits you two could perform."

An angry Ann interceded. "Don't start that again," she warned Louisa.

Roger Twist's six 'colleagues' sat on the back two rows of the second bus. Unlike the angry and confused passengers seated ahead of them, the six were deep in quiet conversation.

"What kind of first class arrangements do you call this?" Moon, the producer, complained.

"Roger wouldn't stand for our being delegated to the **back** of this crowded bus! Just wait 'til he hears about this!"

"Where **is** Roger?" asked Babbs, his personal secretary. "When they announced there was an emergency, I must have fainted for a moment."

"Probably wet your tighty-whities, too," Gloria, the aspiring leading lady, guffawed. "I've been looking for Roger since we hit the ground. No luck.

"My thong may have ended up in his coat pocket," Gloria opined as she reapplied lip-gloss.

"Yeah, where is Roger?" Perry, the tax expert, craned his neck, searching for Twist in the front of the bus. "I thought I saw him enter the escape chute a couple of people ahead of me."

Oliver, the screenwriter/novelist, yawned. "I bet his accommodations are better than these. I last saw him with that Kokk fellow next to the cockpit door."

"That's right," Moon nodded energetically. "I saw him with Kokk, too. Wonder where they are?"

"And the two of them were trailed by that cute airlines girl. I think her name is Janie," Babbs recalled.

"So…we're all in agreement? Nobody knows Roger's whereabouts?" All six nodded.

"So be it," someone whispered.

Just then louder, anguished noises erupted from the front of the bus. "Look! They're unloading our baggage on the ground!"

A lady, pale face pressed against a bus window, shrieked. "Those nasty dogs are smelling my Louis Vuitton cases! How disgusting!"

With a resigned look, an older man sat back in his bus seat. "Appears to me that we're spending the night in this place," he declared.

The lady sitting behind him leaned forward for a better look. "Where are we, anyway? Doesn't look like Pasadena."

Pushing past Louisa, a determined Janie got off the bus and began walking toward the airfield office where she'd seen Kokk enter.

"I'm going to find Jan Kokk. He'll know what's going on."

SEVENTEEN

Some ten miles northwest of the airfield, a worried YO Hotel manager was issuing orders in a manner like those of Sheriff Swartz.

"I want all the hotel staff here for a meeting! Right away! This is an emergency!"

What staff available at that late hour soon arrived, standing or sitting uncomfortably near the front desk as George Aspinwall, manager of Kerrville's YO Ranch Resort Hotel, stepped forward.

His normal concierge-like appearance, black suit, white shirt, black tie and polished tassel loafers accented his nervousness. His manner exclaimed excitement.

"Just had word from the airfield," he shook a paper in the air, his dark locks trembling.

"A planeload of passengers is coming here within minutes. Their plane was forced to make an emergency landing and they're going to spend at least one night with us at the YO. And we're going to show them the Texas hospitality for which the old YO is famous.

"Now," he referred to his notes. "There are 164 of them wanting lodging and a breakfast first thing in the morning. They may leave tomorrow," Aspinwall smiled for the first time, "if their plane is airworthy.

"On the other hand, they may be with us all tomorrow, maybe even tomorrow night.

"Now this is not like a preplanned three-day conference for the rodeo association. We must be highly flexible," he raised his hand dramatically while searching their faces.

"Freddie," he addressed his hotelier. "We need to call in all your extra help. Our guests can double up, two to a room or larger if it's a family.

"We'll let the passengers double up among themselves. You take their names, assign the rooms and hand them their keys.

"They'll arrive shortly in four buses and Eric," he nodded to an assistant, "will line up the buses in the east parking lot where their baggage will be assembled. We'll billet them in buildings 4, that's the

'Colorado;' building 5, 'Paint Creek;' and building 6, 'Johnson Fork.' We'll also need some rooms in building 7, 'Red River.'

"Overflow will go to building 2, the 'Pecos.' That's a good place to assign the aircrew of eight," Aspinwall winked, "since they tend to get pretty rowdy around midnight."

"Unless you have a quick question, Freddie? Enough to keep you busy? Then, go!

"Now, Letticia," he pointed to the restaurant manager. "Same drill for you. Call in extra help now to arrange for the 6:30 morning buffet in the Branding Iron dining room. You'll also need to set up extra tables and seating in the Guadalupe room. Okay?

"I understand the passengers have been fed an evening meal on the plane but we must be ready to provide a la carte and room service until 10:00 this evening."

Aspinwall sighed. "I think that about covers it unless…. Yes, Letticia?"

"What about overtime?"

He clapped his hands together. "Yes, overtime will be authorized. Remember, managers. *Judicious* overtime."

EIGHTEEN

Eyes snapping, Janie stepped inside the airport office building. She slowed, approaching a khaki-clad deputy in the corridor, demanding, "Where's Mr. Kokk?"

"The big man," she added to counter the deputy's bewildered look.

He pointed toward an office door, managing a stern "But you can't go in there, ma'am!"

She paused, hand on the doorknob.

"Why not?"

"Please, ma'am," adroitly he stepped in front of her. "Want me to lose my job? There's a big meeting going on in there."

"Then get Mr. Kokk out here to see me or I'm bargin' in." She threatened to pound her fist on the door.

"Okay, okay," the deputy conceded. "I'll see what I can do," he stepped inside.

Moments later, Kokk emerged from the meeting, notebook in hand. Seeing Janie, he smiled with relief.

She grabbed his free arm. "Happy to see me?"

"Yes! I was afraid you were detained for a statement."

"Well…." She backed off to study him. "**I** was afraid you'd been arrested by one of these Texas cowboys with the big six-shooters."

She side-eyed the deputy standing nearby.

Kokk hugged her. "Not yet. I'm apparently a star witness so far."

"What's going on, Jan?"

He grinned at her ease with his first name. "The Texas Rangers arrived and took over the investigation from the sheriff. The Rangers decided to unload all the baggage, requiring we spend the night here.

"Then the FBI arrived to take charge and decided the plane and the two restrooms would have to be re-examined.

"You're to spend the night in a local hotel as soon as they release your baggage."

"Will you have to be here long?"

Kokk glanced at the closed door. "I'm about to repeat what the late Mr. Twist told me about the people seated in first class. I may be here for a couple more hours."

Kokk squeezed her arm. "You're all right, aren't you? All this excitement doesn't dull your sparkle a bit."

"I'm fine," she blinked demurely. "Just worried that you'd been arrested as a murder suspect.

"And to remind you that you offered me a dinner tonight. Late will be fine. Any restaurant will do."

"I hadn't forgotten," he snorted.

"Just so it doesn't slip your mind, I'm branding you."

She leaned forward to kiss his cheek. "Consider yourself branded, Jan Kokk.

"Here's my cell phone number," she handed him a card. "See you later."

NINETEEN

FBI Special Agent Westbrook's day had been a downer. Called out of an earlier meeting in Dallas, he received a frantic order to investigate a bombing threat on a Boeing 737 just landed in Kerrville. Hastily he assembled a team of available agents, purchased counter tickets at the DFW airport and flew everyone to San Antonio.

There the local FBI agent rented cars for the five people in Westbrook's team. They drove the sixty-two miles westward to Kerrville in the Texas Hill Country.

Now they sat in the small office of the airport manager. There was hardly enough room for the FBI team in addition to the Texas Rangers, sheriff deputies, city police chief and airport manager. Extra folding chairs crowded the four walls of the office. The heat rose exponentially with the number of attendees.

Westbrook's stature compared to the taller Rangers and sheriff deputies didn't bother him. His dark three-piece suit, button-down shirt, wrinkled tie and shiny shoes set him apart from the large strangers surrounding the table. He was used to it.

His angst rose when the foreign private investigator on Flight 236 suddenly was called out of the room. The investigator, named Kokk, was from the Caribbean island of Curacao.

Westbrook stared through bifocals as Kokk returned to the meeting. There was a smudge of lipstick on Kokk's cheek. Westbrook sighed, wiping his glasses with a handkerchief.

Hooks, the Texas Ranger captain, stood. "I think it would be useful for us if Mr. Kokk reviewed his information about the six passengers accompanying the deceased in the first class compartment.

"Mr. Kokk?"

"Thank you," he started thumbing his notebook pages. "In no particular sequence, the deceased, Roger Twist, criticized each of his 'companions.' Companions is my word, certainly not his. Twist had low regard for the six people traveling with him on his dime.

"Please regard my comments and opinions as private and confidential as you would in any investigation. Also remember I'm repeating the words of the deceased, some of which may be true, others may not.

"Twist didn't consider the six his friends. He saw them as employees or business associates whom he generously financed."

At Kokk's nod, a photograph of Moon was projected on the office wall. "These photos were provided just now by personnel from the Sheriff's Department. Thank you, Sheriff.

"Twist's association with Mr. Moon, shown here, was longer than the others. The two of them were successful in writing and producing a hit movie entitled *The Seventh Wife*. Apparently Twist did not consider Moon a friend.

"That film was a success both at the 1983 Cannes Film Festival and in American box offices. Moon was the director and producer, working in tandem with Twist.

"Is this too much detail, ladies and gentlemen?" Kokk asked. Several of the audience shook their heads.

A Texas Ranger sitting beside the sheriff raised a hand. "I don't understand, Mr. Kokk. If Twist and Moon made lots of money together, why any animosity between them?"

"Twist told me that Moon blamed him for the accidental death of Moon's wife long ago. He said he anticipated Moon would eventually 'pay him back' for her death."

Another nod and Oliver's photo was flashed against the wall.

Wetting his thumb, Kokk turned a notebook page. "Mr. Oliver, here, is a famous Hollywood movie critic as well as writer. He collaborated with Twist on many of his films. Twist hoped Oliver's favorable and frequent reviews of his next project would skyrocket the movie's success.

"Despite his anticipation of highly favorable reviews from Oliver of his new work, Twist was highly critical of Oliver's abilities."

Another hand was in the air.

"Yes?" Kokk acknowledged the questioner.

"Even if Oliver knew that, was it enough motive to murder his patron?"

"Good question," Kokk conceded. He raised his large hands in a who-knows gesture. "Twist seemed to think so. Remember, he was paranoid--my opinion--about every one of these six people.

"This next photo is of the lady Twist called Babbs, his personal secretary for many years. She was responsible for his calendar, office and personal expenses.

"Here, as with the previous people, bad feelings existed between the boss and his secretary. One of Babbs' relatives used to work for Twist. This cousin reportedly sold data about Twist's firm to several of his competitors. Twist found out about it and fired him.

"Since then Twist distrusted Babbs. He said she, in turn, hated him since the firing of her favorite cousin.

"Next photo, please." Kokk signaled the operator.

"Here's a glamour shot of the second female in the group of six suspects."

Sheriff Swartz interrupted. "They aren't suspects yet, Kokk."

"Point taken, Sheriff," Kokk conceded. "That depends upon the combined investigation of all you seated here."

Gloria's bikini photo appeared on the wall and several deputies choked, refraining from appreciative whistling.

"This is Gloria's photo," Kokk grinned at their reactions, "not recently but as she appeared in her last film called *Gambol in Vegas*. By the way, Mr. Oliver, one of the six, wrote that screenplay.

"There is a personal relationship between Twist, the movie magnate, and Gloria, this aspiring, ambitious actress. You can draw your own conclusions from what they did in mid-air this afternoon.

"Together they entered the forward restroom of the aircraft. After an appropriate delay, they emerged.

"The restroom was the same one in which Twist was discovered dead several hours later."

Several hands raised simultaneously. "What was the time of death?"

Quickly on his feet, the sheriff was first to answer. "Doctor Harrell, our ME, estimates the time of death was 7:00 p.m."

"Thank you, Sheriff," Westbrook said. "A very important point."

"Next is Mr. Perry," Kokk nodded and Perry's photo was projected on the wall.

"This man is Twist's tax expert in matters both personal and corporate. According to Twist, Perry is acquainted with all the non-tax events buried in Twist's backyard."

Kokk checked his notes to get the words right, "Twist claimed that Perry formerly ran a tax service of questionable integrity in Westwood. I believe that's in the greater Los Angeles area.

"That covers the six people in Twist's party except for Robert, his personal assistant. I learned a new American word yesterday, which seems to accurately describe Robert's duties. He was Twist's 'go-fer.'

"Robert's job ranged from mixing drinks, serving food and handling luggage to coordinating transportation for his boss.

"So that's the gist of what Roger Twist confided to me on the airplane a few hours ago. The six people seated with him in first class were the only passengers allowed in that section per his insistence."

FBI Special Agent Westbrook swung his chair away from the table. "And you think the person who created the bomb threat subsequently murdered Twist in the ensuing confusion of the emergency landing?"

Swartz was on his feet. "The ME hasn't ruled this a homicide. And I emphasize that Kokk's impressions of what Twist said are not evidence."

Westbrook scratched his head. "That's true, Sheriff, but it's a starting point for our investigators. Have you a better one?"

The sheriff sat back down.

"I agree," Ranger Captain Hooks slapped the table. "I suggest, Agent Westbrook, that we form combined teams of our investigators. Let's begun interrogating these six people right away before they can compare or confuse their individual stories."

Westbrook glanced at his watch. "They're probably on their way to a hotel in Kerrville by now."

Turning from the sheriff and captain, Westbrook pointed. "Mr. Kokk?"

Kokk stood beside the door. "Yes?"

"Your opinion?"

"Captain Hooks has an excellent suggestion. May I add a thought?

"The six should be separated and interviewed individually to minimize their exchanging views. The sooner, the better."

TWENTY

Smoking his retrieved pipe, Kokk waited outside the manager's office. Holding his recovered valise, he stood beside one of the sheriff deputies.

The deputy asked, "Ever been to Texas before?"

Kokk admitted this was his first time. "Texas seems very large. Took the plane as long to get here as to get to Miami from Curacao."

"You're from Curacao?"

"That's right."

The deputy grinned and held out his hand. "John Rabe. This is a first for me, too. I've never met anyone from Curacao. In the West Indies, right?"

"Right again. I'm Jan Kokk."

"Oh," Rabe stepped back. "I heard the sheriff talking about you."

Kokk tamped out the pipe. "Think I'd rather not hear what he said."

Rabe grinned. "Yes, sir."

"But I don't mind asking you where is this YO Hotel? That's where all passengers are spending the night."

"It's right on the outskirts of Kerrville, Mr. Kokk. I'm heading back to the office. Why don't I drop you off there on my way?"

"Sounds like you'd better clear that with the sheriff. He might not cotton to that idea. Isn't that a Texas expression?"

--

Arguing with Captain Hooks about guarding the aircraft overnight, Sheriff Swartz's anger increased at the deputy's question about giving Kokk a ride to the hotel.

"Let him take a damn taxi! Deputy, I'm putting you on a patrol of West Kerr County effective right now. You don't have time to show any foreigners the sights of Kerrville."

The sheriff inserted a fresh cigar in his mouth and began chewing. "Understand?"

"Yes, sir."

--

An official black and white SUV later pulled up to Kokk standing beside hangar 1. Deputy Rabe rolled down the window.

"Get in, Mr. Kokk," he called softly.

Kokk crawled into the front seat with Rabe. "Thanks for the ride. I'm not getting you in trouble with your boss, am I?"

The deputy blushed. "Well, just a bit, sir. Please don't tell anyone how you got to the YO tonight."

The time was 10:30 according to Kokk's gold pocket watch. "Is it really so late?" he asked. "Or have I mixed the time zones?"

"It's 10:30, Mr. Kokk."

It was so dark that little scenery could be seen. In minutes, the SUV passed a tall building on their right. "That's the VA Medical Center," Rabe volunteered.

They veered northward off the main road and onto a four-lane.

Rabe, acting like a tour guide, announced, "This is called Veterans Highway and it goes right by your hotel, the YO."

Approaching a major intersection minutes later, they turned into a parking lot. Overhead was a tall obelisk of stones, surmounted by the towering initials YO. A giant letter Y was mounted above an oval-shaped O.

Kokk craned to see the top. "That some kind of monument?"

"No sir. That's just the YO Hotel's sign. See," Rabe pointed upward to the red-rimmed initials. "The YO is shaped like the cattle brand of the old YO ranch famous hereabouts."

Kokk gaped. "If the hotel's as big as its brand, the place must be huge."

"Thanks for the ride, Deputy Rabe. Hope you're not in trouble for bringing me here." They shook hands as Kokk slid out the passenger door, dragging his big leather valise.

Having arrived well after the busloads of passengers, he immediately checked-in at the imposing front desk inside the portico entry.

Following instructions, he found his assigned room in the next door building marked 'Red River.' Kokk tossed the valise on a vacant bed. From the luggage stacked in the corner, he knew he shared the place with a roommate.

"Maybe one of the six people in Twist's group?" he mused aloud. *Hope they're being interviewed already by the investigator teams.*

He unpacked the valise, carefully removing the big bottle of cognac he habitually carried on trips. Finding a water glass in the bathroom, he poured himself a hearty tot. Settling himself on a loveseat, he dialed Janie's cell phone.

"It's Jan," he began when she answered.

"I know your voice." Her reply made him smile. "Where are you?"

"Just arrived at the hotel. Care to have dinner with a lonely old private investigator from faraway Curacao?"

Her voice was crisp as if she'd preplanned what to say. "Meet you by the big bear in fifteen minutes?"

"Where?" Kokk contained himself from answering 'Huh?' It was an American word he had just learned.

"By the big bear in the lobby. See you in fifteen."

Chuckling, he turned off the cell phone, took a quick shower and donned a fresh shirt from the valise.

He enjoyed the cognac, then ambled back toward the massive lobby. Finding the big stuffed bear was easy. It dominated the huge lobby.

Kokk sat down and began composing a message to his friend, Police Chief van Hooser in Curacao.

"Unavoidably detained by the emergency landing of my airplane in Texas. The landing here is complicated by a bomb threat plus a murder. I'll continue my assignment as soon as possible. Will contact you when I arrive in Los Angeles."

--

Special Agent Westbrook, Texas Ranger Captain Hooks and Sheriff Swartz pulled up chairs to the green-clothed dining table set up for them in the YO's Spanish Oak room.

In the other three corners of the large room, uniformed officers prepared to interview and take statements from the six first class passengers. The investigators had agreed on an easy title, 'The Sixers,' for the group.

In the adjoining Cypress meeting room, city police were assisting the interrogators by segregating 'The Sixers' in widely spaced chairs on the facing wall. The chairs were far enough to discourage exchanges.

Were that not enough, a stern police sergeant sat near the door holding a roster of their names. Another policewoman would escort each called person to the appropriate table for interview in the next room.

Not even a hot cup of YO coffee could appease the testy sheriff. "I don't like it," he spilled coffee on the green tablecloth.

Hooks and Westbrook nodded at each other, guessing what would follow.

"This guy Kokk has no business being included in the interviews. He's just a homegrown private investigator with zero, zero," he repeated, "official standing here.

"He's even a foreigner! For all we know, he could be the perpetrator or honcho of this entire mess."

Westbrook interrupted the tirade. "We're already checking on his bona fides, Sheriff. We're making sure he's who he claims to be."

"Sheriff, you've got to admit that Kokk's been cooperative and very useful so far." Hooks looked at Westbrook for agreement.

"Without his presence on the flight and observations, we'd still be scrambling."

Shaking his head, Swartz frowned at both of them. "I don't like it one bit.

"I want to go on the record that allowing Kokk to sit in, observe--or whatever--these official interviews is a big mistake."

"Noted," Westbrook said flatly. He turned to one of his agents. "Go find Mr. Kokk and ask him to join us here."

--

Blinking, Kokk eased himself into a big cowhide sofa while admiring the cavernous lobby as he waited for Janie. The giant, high ceiling, joist-roofed interior reminded him of an old fashioned hunting lodge. The walls were covered with dozens of mounted trophies of exotic animals.

"Prince Rudolph's royal lodge at Mayerling must have looked like this," he mused aloud.

In middle of the floor stood a preserved standing brown bear, at least twelve feet tall in an angry fighting pose.

How did I possibly miss that monster when I registered at the front desk? he wondered.

Suddenly, Janie, dressed in a black cocktail dress and pearls, approached. She immediately stopped any interest in the bear.

He arose and hugged her. "Is this what you Americans call a bear hug?"

Delighted, she bussed his cheek.

"Care for a drink?" Kokk pointed to the entrance to the Elm Water Hole bar on the far side of the lobby. "Or we could have one with dinner."

"We'd better go in before they close the restaurant over there," she pointed in the opposite direction.

"See its name?" she gloated. 'Branding Iron.' That's why I branded you earlier," she gushed.

Inside the almost deserted dining area, they claimed a corner table. "Tell me what you've been doing, Mr. Famous PI."

He liked her panache. "Talking to the assorted law enforcement officials suddenly gathered here like buzzards, lovely inquiring lady."

He patted a pocket of his coat. "Mind if I smoke my pipe?"

"I'd be delighted but smoking isn't allowed in most restaurants, Jan. Just like on the airplane."

"Then I'll need a drink for certain," he replaced the pipe and they ordered drinks from the nearby waitress.

"You have a roommate, too?" Kokk asked.

"Yes, all the crew does. Ann and I are stabled together in Pecos, the farthest building. You're also sharing a room?"

He nodded. "But I have no idea who he is. The room was vacant except for a pile of masculine-type luggage in the corner."

As the drinks arrived, he suggested they order from the leather-cased menus handed them.

"The shrimp are from the Gulf?" Janie asked.

"The shrimp salad should be very good," she added as the waitress nodded. "I'll bet you're starving, Jan. Texas is famous for its steaks."

"No," he shook his head. "I'm good."

To the waitress, he turned. "Shrimp salads for both of us. And more drinks, please."

Janie straightened the pearls tangled during the bear hug. "Do you think we'll fly out of here in the morning?"

Kokk examined, then patted her hand. "No idea. They need the medical examiner's report to determine if Twist's demise was a homicide or not.

"If it is, I can't imagine they'll allow all their witnesses to disappear into the western sky."

She placed a hand on his cuff. "I want to hear about your legendary exploits solving cases all over the Caribbean. For starts, have you always lived in Curacao?"

"Most of my life," he acknowledged. "But you're not getting off that easy, Janie Roland.

"First, tell **me** where you grew up, went to school, became a flight attendant. And," he blinked his eyes at her expression, "when's your planned marriage?"

"It'll take more than a shrimp salad and two martinis for me to confess all that," she chided. "You go first."

"Okay," he smiled broadly. "Does 'okay' have an American or Texan provenance?"

She made a face. "Stop evading. Tell me about you, evasive pirate."

Kokk sat back. "You sound like one of my instructors back in crime school."

"That's a small start. Tell me. Talk."

"I attended police academy in Curacao at an early age. Now it's your turn."

"I went to school at Oklahoma State University. That's in Oklahoma, just north of Texas," she elaborated at his look.

"What happened after the police academy? Did you serve in the local police?"

"Those green eyes are really splendid," he substituted a more appealing subject.

Janie glowered, pursing her lips.

"All right," he relented. "Yes, I was a policeman in Curacao for two years, then volunteered for training in the Netherlands. Ever been there?"

"Not yet," she emphasized as if she had plans. "What kind of training?"

"I enlisted in the Royal Dutch Gendarmerie."

"What's that?"

"I don't think there's an American equivalent. It's sort of a national military police."

"Continue, please."

"First, aren't you going to tell me what you studied at the university? It's your turn."

"Political science. How long did you live in the Netherlands?"

"Only a short time. My unit went to Surinam as peace-keepers. I was wounded, discharged and sent back home to Curacao.

"Now, why did you change horses from political science--whatever that is--to aviation?"

Abruptly, Kokk sat up, alerted. A dark-suited man approached them. "Mr. Kokk?"

Kokk glanced up, recognizing the dark suit, white shirt and tie as the bureau standard. "Yes?"

"Sorry for the interruption, sir. Special Agent Westbrook asks you to come with me now. Extremely urgent, sir."

Kokk tittered sadly at Janie. "I'll pay the check. Please excuse me and enjoy your meal."

Sighing, he rose from the table. Suddenly animated, he asked, "Can we meet here for an early--hopefully undisturbed--breakfast in the morning?"

"I'll be here, Jan. Six o'clock too early?"

"Perfect," he agreed.

He bent over and kissed her forehead. "Now you're branded, too. I'll expect an answer about that planned date for your marriage at this very same table at six."

Winking at her expression, he dutifully followed the FBI agent out the door of the Branding Iron.

TWENTY ONE

Morosely, Kokk tamped out the burned residue of his little black pipe against the arm of the old fashioned rocking chair in which he sat. His motion made the chair near the hotel's front entrance teeter.

He'd been unable to sleep once he returned to his room at four this autumn morning. His mind refused to surrender the continuing tumble of information he'd heard after leaving Janie.

Another deterrent was his roommate's snoring. The loud wheezing defied slumber. Although difficult to recognize in the bed linens, the roommate looked like Perry, the tax expert of Twist's six-person coterie of Hollywood hangers-on.

Kokk wondered if any of those six people genuinely regretted Twist's death. Perhaps they all had acted in concert to kill him, like the passengers on Agatha's famous *Orient Express*.

To fill the hour until he met Janie for breakfast. Kokk trimmed his graying mustache. Then he shaved carefully, wondering why beards seemed to be vogue among American males.

Kokk saw a fleck of shaving foam in one ear missed by the towel. He blotted clean a razor nick on the chin.

Has Janie already noticed my several impediments? He hoped not as he leaned back in the rocker.

Across the street was an emerald green hill topped by a large American flag curling in the morning breeze. Near the flag, but on a higher local precipice was a towering cross, outlined by its reddish steel skeleton.

Texans liked big things, he reminded himself, briefly shutting his eyes, imagining what Janie's morning mood would be.

The rolling green hills, still misted by scattered clouds, seemed peaceful, unlike the madcap airport scene. Kokk wondered if he could have slept out of doors instead of in the small room dominated by a snoring roommate.

Sighing, Kokk checked the big gold pocket watch. "Time to go," he said aloud to cajole himself out of the chair and back into the hotel.

64

Janie saw him first and wagged her hand excitedly as if he might miss her. "Good morning, Jan."

He bent over and kissed her cheek. "You look as enticing as you did last night," he exclaimed. "What's your secret? I must look as frazzled and worn as yesterday's newspaper."

"I'm just happy to see you," she gushed, hoping she wasn't blushing.

"A buffet is prepared in the Guadalupe room over there," she gestured. "Or would you prefer…"

"Finding you here, at last night's table, is perfect," he assured her, wagging at the waiter for coffee. "I apologize for last night's interruption. Today I want you all to myself. Notice that the action verb is 'want.'"

Unable to withhold more blush, she grinned like a schoolgirl. "You have me, unless the airline intervenes."

The caveat changed her expression. "Is it likely that we'll be on our way to LA this morning?"

"Not a chance." He cradled her hand as coffee was served, accompanied by two tall menus.

Squeezing his hand, she guessed. "The medical examiner's report?"

"Exactly. The ME did his job unexpectedly fast, probably encouraged by the FBI presence. It was delivered while I was sitting in the interrogations early this morning. The FBI guy invited me to observe.

"The ME found the cause of Twist's death was a poison--possibly strychnine—but definitely not a heart attack."

"Murder he wrote?"

Kokk stirred the coffee and sipped appreciatively. "Yes, murder. So the FBI and others won't allow the flight to resume until they've run more checks on all the passengers."

"And crew?"

"Yes, love. And crew. They want to check fingerprints for lipstick residues from the restroom mirror you showed me."

"Well," she demurred. "The culprit could have scrubbed his hands clean by now."

Kokk nodded agreement. "A little late, aren't they?"

Chin on fist, Janie leaned forward. "What about the murder? Has Sam Spade ferreted any leads as yet?"

Conversation slowed as they ordered Belgian waffles and sausages. "More coffee, please," Kokk reminded the waiter.

As the waiter scurried off, Kokk leaned closer. "Also they want the hands of those six people in first class tested for possible traces of poison. If those first six prove negative, then they'll check rest of us."

"Wow," she exclaimed. "We'll be standing in line all day!"

"I hope you have no background record of murder or mayhem? The sheriff already suspects that I do," Kokk chuckled.

Janie's mood changed so suddenly, he stifled his mirth. "Something wrong?"

A dark-suited, official looking man approached their table. This time the agent stood aside, motioning for Kokk to follow.

"Uh-oh. Will we never have any privacy?" Kokk snorted as he stood.

"When's your planned wedding? I have that and several other topics I want to hear about."

He bent to kiss her cheek. "Plus a suggestion about tonight's activities. Guess I'll have to catch up with you later for answers."

TWENTY TWO

A sheriff-marked SUV waited out front, Deputy Rabe at the wheel. Kokk and the FBI agent clambered in.

"Good morning, Deputy," Kokk tried to mask his irritation at being called away. "Where are we going?"

"Back to the airport, Mr. Kokk."

The agent next to Kokk yawned, then leaned forward.

"Faster," he urged the deputy. "I guarantee you won't get a speeding ticket," he kidded.

This time Highway 27 was free of stalled traffic and parked vehicles along the sides of the road. Once inside the airport gate, the SUV slowed because the narrow airport access road was clogged with TV vans festooned with tall antennas.

"Looks like the press and television heard about the bomb threat and the murder?"

"News like that travels fast," the FBI agent agreed. "A press conference is planned out here for ten o'clock. We've even added a visiting dignitary from the Homeland Security Department."

The Boeing 737 sat forlornly in the same spot as yesterday, main door open and staircase ramp in place.

The agent pointed to the open door of the plane as the SUV braked to a stop. "They want you up there, Mr. Kokk."

--

Kokk carefully limped up the staircase and was immediately beckoned inside. "Morning, Mr. Kokk," another agent, whose nametag read 'KORF,' welcomed him aboard.

"Special Agent Westbrook wanted you to see a couple of things in here before meeting with him and Captain Hooks in the office.

"The sheriff, too?" Kokk wanted to know.

"Yes, sir. The sheriff, too. And a just-arrived officer from Homeland Security."

As they walked down the aisle to the rear of the plane, Kokk was handed plastic gloves which, with effort, he slipped on his hands.

"We lifted lots of prints from this restroom where the bomb threat was scribbled on the mirror. We've looked all over for the lipstick used to write the threat. Nothing."

"Did you check the toilet holding tank?"

"Yes, sir. No luck," he shook his head. "Now may we go back to the front and look at the other restroom?

"Captain Hooks thought you'd be particularly interested in what we found up there."

Holding up a clear evidence bag containing some powder, Korf pointed. "We found a tiny spill of an alkaloid on the carpeting in here."

Kokk glanced at the bag. "I'm guessing you disassembled the light fixtures, looked under the counter, everywhere, and found nothing?"

"Correct."

Kokk studied the walls. "No place to hide anything in here is there?"

"If there were," Korf smiled, "we'd have found it. Now I'm to escort you over to the airport office where the others are meeting."

Pulling off the gloves, Kokk tossed them into a disposal sack. "Thanks for showing me what the techs have been doing. I can find my way to the office. What's brewing over there?"

Agent Korf held up four figures. "Meeting of the big four: FBI, Homeland Security, Texas Rangers and the local Sheriff Department."

Korf grinned broadly. "By now they've decided who speaks and who listens at the ten o'clock press conference. In your absence, they may have elected you as chief spokesman, Mr. Kokk."

Kokk bellowed. "I've been to too many press conferences. I know civilians from out of town--like me--are invited only to flesh-out the audience."

Laughing, they parted and Kokk walked over to the airport manager's office. An obliging deputy held the office door for him.

Inside, only four men sat at the formerly crowded table. "Come in, Mr. Kokk, and meet Mr. Dan Roe of the Homeland Security Department. He's just arrived from Washington."

Shifting in his chair, Westbrook watched the two men shake hands. Kokk took the remaining chair beside Sheriff Swartz, who stared straight ahead.

Westbrook explained to Roe. "Mr. Kokk is the investigator from Curacao who was on the airplane. Lucky for us. His observations about the bomb threat and later murder have been most useful.

"He's just seen the two crime scenes on the aircraft as you did. Any comments, Mr. Kokk?"

Kokk cleared his throat, wishing he'd brought his pipe. "Nothing of significance, I'm sure," he began.

At this, Sheriff Swartz glanced at Kokk for the first time.

Kokk continued. "At the back restroom of the plane, it might be useful if you could determine if any of the many fingerprints there are from passengers in the first class section. Usually the first classers would use the forward restroom. If first class fingerprints were found in the rear restroom, they might identify who wrote the threat on the mirror."

"That's a waste of time, Kokk," Swartz spoke up. "There is no reason to think someone from first class walked to the rear and scribbled that threat on the mirror. Why link the person writing the threat in the rear of the plane with the death of someone in the forward first class section?"

"Death or murder?"

Before the sheriff could respond, Kokk continued. "The sheriff has a point. Maybe these were two completely unrelated incidents? But in my limited experience, such coincidence is suspicious." Kokk tousled his hair.

"May I also suggest," he added, "that the two ladies seated in first class be interrogated, if they haven't been already, about Twist's medications? He told me he was taking a yellow capsule called digitoxin for blood pressure."

Ranger Captain Hooks nodded while making another note. "He means the ladies we've been calling Babbs and Gloria," he explained to Roe.

"Why your suggestion, Mr. Kokk?" Roe wondered aloud.

Kokk rubbed his eyes. "As Twist's personal assistant, Babbs meted out his medication, if I recall correctly.

"Gloria, the aspiring movie star, was in the restroom with Twist yesterday afternoon. He told me he secreted two of his capsules in that restroom to take in case of an emergency."

"Also a good point," Westbrook made a note of his own.

He pyramided his fingers. "The ME says Twist died of poison. Maybe one or both of those females know how poison could have gotten mixed with or substituted for the prescribed digitoxin he was taking?"

"I see no harm in checking the fingerprints of the back restroom to see if any of them are from our 'sixers.'

"Let's immediately arrange for interview of the two ladies. Mr. Kokk, could you again sit in on those interviews as an observer?

"We need to solve this case expeditiously and get the innocent passengers out of here."

"Amen to that!" Airport manager Mitchell exclaimed.

The sheriff stood suddenly, upending a folding chair as he stormed out of the office.

TWENTY THREE

Four large television vans formed a semicircle around airport hangar number 2. Their crews began connecting cables and equipment in front of a line of yellow tape separating them from a microphone erected in front of the hangar. Well beyond the cameras and crews sat the Boeing 737 still cordoned off by police.

"Mike Kirby here reporting from Kerrville for WOAI, San Antonio, on the emergency landing last evening of a commercial aircraft, Southwestern Flight 236 carrying 164 passengers and crew. The reason for the emergency landing at the Kerrville-Kerr County Airport was a bomb threat discovered on the aircraft.

"Shortly before the plane safely landed without any reported injuries, a body was discovered in one of the aircraft's restrooms. The identity of the person has not yet been publicly announced pending next of kin notification. The fatality is under investigation, as is the hoax bomb threat.

"This press conference called by law enforcement officials, including the FBI and Texas Rangers, will begin in a few minutes. We anticipate those officials will explain these incidents and if terrorism is suspected."

Inside the manager's office angry voices wavered upon hearing the booming voice of the television commentator outside. Special Agent Westbrook stood near the head of the table. Seated around him were Texas Ranger Captain Hooks, Mr. Roe of Homeland Security and an unhappy Sheriff Swartz.

"The FBI is in charge of this investigation, Sheriff, as well as the press conference we're about to begin."

Westbrook passed out several typed sheets. "For the conference, I'm providing each of you sample remarks you may use when you speak to the press outside. **Sample** remarks," he repeated, looking again at Swartz.

"These remarks are a simple outline of the problem and what we're doing to determine the identity of the perpetrator or perpetrators of the bomb threat and the murder of a passenger."

Roe raised a hand. "Is the public invited or just the press?"

Westbrook shook his head. "No. I decided to allow only the TV and press representatives onto the airport. We still have crime scenes being worked here."

Roe nodded at the explanation.

"I plan to begin by introducing each of you," Westbrook adjusted his tie, "then calling on you for remarks. Please use your samples.

"Here's the order I intend to ask you to speak. First, Sheriff Swartz, as the head local law enforcement representative, then Captain Hooks and lastly Mr. Roe.

"Please," Westbrook studied Swartz again. "Be concise since there's not much we can reveal at this point about our **joint** investigation. Talking points are summarized in your sample remarks.

"Please be collegial. We're handling a complex problem very well considering it's early times. After our brief remarks, we'll allow questions. I'll call upon each of you to answer those queries which seem appropriate to you."

A hand was raised. "Do the Q&A include Mr. Kokk?"

A frowning sheriff stood. "If so, I decline to take part." He plopped back down.

"No," Westbrook answered evenly. "Mr. Kokk is not here officially, despite our reliance on his observations and advice.

"Other questions, gentlemen?" Westbrook scanned their faces. "Then let's get out there and do as good a job as possible considering the short period of our investigation."

On the way out the door, Captain Hooks cornered the sheriff. "Ride easy, Sheriff. I'm sure you didn't mean your little threat about not participating. My department would not be favorably impressed. The same goes for your voters, I think."

Swartz made no reply.

Television cameras operating, Westbrook, Hooks, Roe and Swartz stepped up to positions marked with their names.

Westbrook introduced, then spelled each of their names for the benefit of the dozen reporters and TV commentators. After the four officials made remarks, Westbrook called for questions.

"Just a few," he posited. "We have lots more to do to complete this investigation."

He recognized a reporter wearing a necktie in the front row.

"Were any explosive devices found on the airplane?"

"None, thank goodness. Speaking of thanks, the Sheriff Departments of Kerr and Kendall Counties are highly commended for their quick and thorough searches, not only of the aircraft but of all the baggage. Thanks also to the Kerrville Police Department for its continuing cooperation and assistance."

Another hand in the air, this one from a young man wearing a plaid jacket. "Who discovered the bomb threat?"

"One of the aircraft crew, a flight attendant."

Another hand came up. "Have you discovered who made the threat? Was it a passenger?"

"Our investigation is proceeding but I have no answer to those questions at this time."

"Who was the dead passenger found after landing?"

Westbrook nodded at Hooks, who responded. "We can't disclose that until next of kin have been notified. We're trying to locate them as we speak."

A female TV commentator wearing slacks asked "Male or female?"

"How's that?"

"Was the dead passenger male or female?"

"Male."

"Was his death the result of the emergency landing?"

Westbrook nodded at Swartz to answer. "No, the death has been ruled a homicide by our county medical examiner."

The audience gasped, encouraging the questioner to add, "Any suspects yet?"

"The investigation is underway. We can't answer that as yet." With a pained expression, Swartz looked up from his reading.

"Where are the passengers?"

Westbrook answered. "They're all safe and resting in a local hotel."

"When will they be allowed to resume travel?"

Again, Westbrook replied. "As soon as our preliminary checks are completed, clearing each passenger."

"Have you identified any 'persons of interest,' if that's the correct phrase, for either the murder or bomb threat?"

Hooks shook his head. "No comment."

A female reporter spoke up. "Are you categorizing the bomb threat or homicide or both as terrorism?"

Roe nodded at her. "We're still in the first phrases of our investigation. Nothing can be ruled out at this early stage."

"Will there be another conference later today? And when can we interview the crew and some of the passengers?"

"To be determined," Westbrook grinned, pleased an end to this conference was in sight.

"We'll let you know where and when. Thank you for attending. Your vans must now leave the airport as we can't provide security for them as well as the crime scenes."

"Thank you again," he waved as the four officials turned around to return to the airport office.

Mike Kirby, the WOAI TV commentator, nudged a colleague as the crowd around the microphone began dispersing.

"Getting answers 'round here is like trying to rope a jack rabbit, ain't it?" he joked in a Texas accent.

"Let's find us a waterin' hole an' rest our hosses," his friend replied in kind.

TWENTY FOUR

While the press conference began outside, three detectives, FBI, Texas Ranger and Sheriff's Department, arranged notepads and recorders in a vacant office. They discussed an interview plan for each of the two females. Jan Kokk sat in the far corner, chagrinned he was neglecting Janie and couldn't even light his pipe.

Agent Daniels took the lead. "The first lady we see is Gloria Denham, the younger of the two. Mr. Kokk, please begin by telling us what you know about Gloria."

"Attractive, ambitious and apparently an intimate friend of the deceased. Gloria hoped to be the leading lady in his next epic movie. She entertained the deceased yesterday afternoon in the airplane's forward restroom."

"Whew," one of the detectives wheezed. "How did they manage anything in such a small space?"

"I'm sure she'd elaborate if you asked nicely," Kokk jested.

He became serious the next moment. "Of significance is that Twist told me he had hidden two of his blood pressure capsules in that same restroom in case he needed an emergency dose."

Another detective spoke up. "Did Gloria know the location of those capsules. Are they still there?"

The Texas Ranger shook his head. "If the capsules were still in the restroom, they would have been found by our crime-scene team."

"Good question," the studious deputy sheriff made herself a note.

"Do we know who used the restroom following their wha-cha-ma-call-it?"

"'Dalliance' seems as good a description as any," volunteered the now smiling female deputy.

"Dalliance, it is." Daniels repeated as they all agreed.

"We don't know who used the restroom between the end of the 'dalliance' and finding the body once the plane landed."

"More good questions." Daniels leaned back. "Anything else? Are we ready to see Gloria?"

Everyone nodded agreement.

Gloria entered the room and seated herself after acknowledging the rights read her by Daniels. She also agreed to the recording of the conversation.

Gloria seemed relaxed, dressed in heels, a short paisley skirt and tan silk blouse.

She studied her questioners, then sighed, not finding one to suit her. Instead she began filing long, polished nails, simultaneously exhibiting several inches of thigh.

"Please put the file away, Miss," Daniels remonstrated. "This is a murder investigation, a very serious business."

Gloria sighed again and shoved the file into an expensive leather handbag.

In answer to questions about the capsules left in the restroom, she didn't hesitate.

"Sure, I saw Roger tape some capsules above the door. He said he might need them in a hurry. Old Babbs, who kept his pills, was too slow in an emergency, he said."

The female deputy leaned over, checking the recorder. "Can you describe the capsules?"

"What do you mean? They were just little capsules. About this long," she held up a finger and thumb. "Yellow ones, I think."

"Did you remove the capsules from above the door?"

"Certainly not," Gloria huffed. "My Roger might have needed them. In the restroom I could tell his heart rate was…up."

"Did you see anyone remove the capsules from the restroom?"

"No."

"Your airplane seat, seat A1, was immediately next to the restroom. Who used the restroom after you and the deceased came out?"

"I don't remember. I was redoing my nails after that. He'd pawed them in there." Poising hands in front of her, Gloria examined the repaired nails.

"Did you tell anyone about the capsules left over the door in the rest room?"

Gloria hesitated. "Sure, I did," she beamed at remembering. "I told Babbs since she keeps track of his pills and things."

"Did you tell anyone else?"

She reached into the handbag. "Mind if I smoke?"

"Sorry. No smoking in here."

Miffed, Gloria eased back into the chair. "Anyone could have heard what I told Babbs. She was standing there, waiting to use the restroom."

"Anyone else standing nearby?"

Gloria plucked a lipstick out of the handbag. "I dunno. Maybe one of the hostesses was there, talking to Robert."

"Could Robert have heard what you said about the capsules?

"Dunno. Maybe."

"Miss, were your hands checked for residue?" As he asked the question, Daniels passed about the negative result of her test.

"Is that what they were doing? I was afraid they'd spoil my nails!"

"Yeah, they put something on my hands, then told me I could wipe it off."

The deputy asked her closing question. "In your opinion, who murdered him, Gloria?"

She shrugged. "It sure wasn't me! Roger was the goose who…."

Suddenly she stopped and substituted, "I mean he was my benefactor." She giggled.

Daniels turned to Kokk sitting in the corner. Kokk answered the look with a shake of the head.

"Thank you for your assistance, Miss. If you think of anything to add to your statement which is being prepared for your signature, please call me immediately." Daniels handed her his card.

"Maybe I will," she tucked the card into her bag. "Maybe I will."

As Gloria flounced out with a backward look at Daniels, the three investigators turned to Kokk expectantly.

"The next lady is Babbs Solomon. She was the personal assistant of the deceased. He told me Babbs was a long-time employee taking care of his calendar, appointments, dictation, typing and office and personal expenses.

"Perhaps unusual, Babbs didn't make travel arrangements for her boss. Robert, his factotum, performed that chore.

"I suggest that Babbs' most significant duty concerning this case was her handing Twist his medication for high blood pressure. It is--rather was--digitoxin, a rather common prescribed remedy I'm told.

"Apparently the relationship between Twist and Babbs was not always happy. In the past Twist fired a favorite cousin of hers for leaking information about his firm to competitors. Since then Twist said he distrusts her. On her part, Babbs very much resented Twist's firing her relative.

"Unlike Gloria, Babbs is mature and quiet. One commonality is their financial dependency on Twist.

"In Babb's case, it was a good, regular salary. I think the glamorous Gloria expected a windfall movie role from the deceased.

"One other point, perhaps minor. Gloria and Babbs were assigned to share a hotel room here. They're roommates."

The Ranger chuckled. "Another *Odd Couple*, would you say?"

A timid knock sounded on the door.

Daniels raised his voice. "Come in, please, Ms. Solomon."

"Thank you for cooperating with our investigation," he began, then pointed. "Please have a seat there."

She sat, looking furtively about the room and at her inquisitors. Daniels read her rights. Then he asked if she consented that the interview be recorded.

The Texas Ranger wasted no time in asking about the prescription drug. "Tell us, please, about your medicinal duties for the late Mr. Twist."

Babbs held her hands tightly clasped, near her chest. She swallowed. "I keep his heart medicine in my desk drawer at work, in Hollywood, you know."

"Yes?"

"Then I give it to Mr. Twist at the hours prescribed by the doctor. Sometimes he asks for a capsule at other times when he feels stressed."

"Please go on. You're doing fine," Daniels attempted to calm her.

"Where do the pills...?"

"They're capsules," Babbs corrected the deputy.

"Thank you. Where do the capsules come from?"

"We--that is, Robert--reorders them by telephone when I ask him. If the prescription needs renewal, Mr. Twist telephones the doctor and Robert goes there to bring it back."

"Can you account for every one of the capsules?"

"Of course. I've done that for years."

Then the Ranger asked, "Did you know Mr. Twist left two capsules in the forward restroom yesterday?"

Babbs shrugged. "He asked for two extras yesterday. I gave them to him and he put them in his shirt pocket."

"Did you know he left them in the restroom?"

She glowered. "Gloria, his current squeeze, told me that."

The deputy sheriff interrupted. "Did Gloria tell you specifically where the pills were in the restroom?"

"No, she didn't."

"Did you see the pills in the restroom when you went in following their--dalliance--in the restroom?"

Babbs' hands trembled. "I don't remember seeing any capsules in there. But I wasn't looking for them, either."

"So you didn't remove them?"

"Certainly not."

It was the FBI investigator's turn. "Did you notice who used the restroom after you?"

"No, I returned to my seat and read a magazine."

"Do you and Gloria get along well?"

Babbs blotted dry lips with a tissue. "Me...I'm just hired help. I have to get along with everyone. Gloria and I are roommates at the moment although she's seldom in the room."

Daniels nodded as he passed out the residue test result on Babbs. "Were your hands tested for residue from the capsules?"

"Yes, sir."

Daniels held up the result. "This says there were traces of poison residue on your hands. Can you explain that?"

She suddenly hung her head, sobbing. "No, I can't! I don't know why! Why do you ask me so many questions?"

The deputy's next question further upset Babbs. "Did you switch Mr. Twist's capsules for something else?"

"No, no, no!"

Kokk leaned forward to offer tissues. A minute later, still sniffling, Babbs stood.

"I'd like to be excused," she croaked as she left the room. "I'm not feeling well."

In unison, the investigators looked at Kokk in the corner. He nodded.

After Babbs left, the Ranger coughed. "I think we ought to see this Robert character as well. Maybe he can shed some light on the medication question."

Everyone at the table nodded. Daniels stood and stretched. "I'll send for him. Let's take a twenty-minute break."

--

Johan Piaker spun about in his leather executive chair on the thirty-fourth floor of the Nation's Bank building in Los Angeles, California. He needed a break--preferably permanent--from his subordinate's terse report and scolding look about the Consulate's overspent finances.

Henri Boudin, Piaker's administrative officer, recited recent unfinanced expenditures to the growing irritation of his supervisor. Piaker's title was Minister Plenipotentiary and Consul General of Curacao to Greater Los Angeles, California, USA.

Piaker thought his impressive title should exempt him from close scrutiny, especially from an youth like Boudin.

"You've already spent $32,000 more than available this quarter," Boudin smirked.

Piaker looked at the younger man over bifocals. This kid wants my job if I'm disgraced and sent home to Curacao, he thought.

Unhappy with the recent downward path of his diplomatic career, Piaker rotated back to stare out the window. Down below, Wilshire Boulevard was a mess. The light at the La Brea intersection was out, resulting in a noisy traffic snarl.

Somehow the honking vehicles and confusion below claimed his attention instead of the irksome budget shortfalls. The shortages were the result of overspending--his own--he admitted. The admin officer's attitude did not amuse his Consul General.

Piaker's superiors back in Willemstad, capital of Curacao, were equally unhappy. The Foreign Secretary, normally a bastion of calm, was angry enough to order Piaker to return home to stand in front of the Secretary's desk.

To insure Piaker's appearance, a detective named Kokk had been dispatched to LA. He would escort Piaker back to Willemstad, willingly or not.

"Heard anything from that Kokk fellow?" Piaker demanded, still concentrating on the traffic.

"Only that his flight's been detained in Texas, sir."

"Has the Ministry replied to any of my requests for supplemental funds?"

Boudin positively leered. "Yes, sir. They turned us down. No more money."

"Not even my representational funds?"

"Yes, sir."

At this Piaker stood up, shaking both fists in the air. "How do they expect me to entertain other diplomats and business visitors without ample funds? Don't they realize that a social get together here in LA costs more--much more--than as simple gathering in Willemstad?

"Go, go!" Piaker waved Boudin out of the room. "Check your books again! There must be some money left somewhere in our quarterly allowances."

Dejected, Piaker resumed the big chair and his vigil over Wilshire. Realizing her husband's recall was imminent, wife Rosa had already left him for Curacao, increasing Piaker's depression.

"No wife, no money," he mused aloud. "And the Minister's sending someone here to take me home like a criminal. I might even be dismissed from the diplomatic service!"

Reaching for the bottom drawer of his desk, he withdrew a liquor bottle. "Hold my calls," he ordered his secretary in the outer office.

"I'm in conference."

TWENTY FIVE

Outside for a breath of air, Kokk dialed Janie's cell phone. She answered immediately. "Where are you? I thought we were having lunch together."

He held the phone in place with a shoulder while extracting his pipe. "I wanted to but I was asked to sit in on some more interviews. They're still ongoing.

"May I offer you a long, uninterrupted dinner interspersed with exotic drinks tonight? Any interest?"

"You bet," she gushed. "How are the interviews going? Anyone in handcuffs yet?"

"They just finished talking to Babbs, Twist's personal secretary. She's very upset and didn't fare too well with the investigators I fear.

"Being good Samaritans, maybe you and Ann could take Babbs to lunch and revive, calm and restore her. It would be a great good deed."

"Wow!" Janie's tone changed. "She must be really bad."

Kokk expertly lit his pipe with a kitchen match. "I'll call you as soon as my timing is more certain. We have a date?"

"Yes, yes, yes! I'll see you later, handsome pirate."

--

Returning to the interrogation room after consuming a large fajita taco, Kokk nodded at Robert standing in the anteroom.

Since the three detectives were already there, he remained standing as he flipped through his notes. "Robert House," he looked up.

"My comments on Robert result from my observation. Twist had little to say about his 'go-fer,' I believe that's the appropriate Texas expression.

"A long time Twist employee--like Babbs--Robert arranges all air and ground transportation for his boss. He mixes and serves drinks, makes snacks, arranges menus and attempts to keep his boss on time to meetings and rehearsals.

"Twist told me there was something in Robert's past which Twist uses--rather used--to Robert's disadvantage. If any of you have a background report on Robert, it would be useful to share it now."

The three detectives shook their heads.

"Seems like an opportune time for me to request I be permitted to read any background reports you," he looked at FBI Agent Daniels, "gather about the first class passengers and the crew of Flight 236."

Daniels nodded, making himself a note.

"I did not realize until Babb's testimony," Kokk reflected, "that Robert obtained refills and requested renewals of Twist's blood pressure medicine. That's worth exploring.

"Sorry that's all I can tell you about your next subject."

"Since you're up, Mr. Kokk, please bring him in," Daniels asked.

Once Robert sat down at the big interview table, Daniels read him his rights and said that their conversation would be recorded.

Robert began with a detailed precis of his duties. He described Roger Twist as a difficult, often temperamental chief.

"Very critical," Robert added at a deputy's question. "He didn't stand for partial answers or half measures.

"Mr. Twist's daily schedule was habitually full and hectic. He angered easily, I would say," Robert sat back in his chair, comfortable with the situation as well as their questions.

The Texas Ranger asked about medications. "Yes, I reordered his prescription when Babbs told me she needed more." At this, Daniels passed out the negative report of the residues on Robert's hands.

"Did you overhear what Gloria said to Babbs outside the restroom?"

Robert countered. "Can you be more specific?"

"She told Babbs about some capsules left in the restroom for emergency use by the deceased."

"Yes, I heard that. So did several others who were standing in the aisle at the time."

"Who were they?"

Robert frowned before replying. "I remember one of the flight attendants. Also, Mr. Moon was there and must have heard what Gloria said."

"Did you enter the restroom and see the capsules left there?"

"No, ma'am."

"Did you remove or replace them?"

Robert stiffened as if affronted. "No, certainly not."

"What will you do now that your employer is dead?" Daniels rubbed his chin.

Robert shook his head. "I'll have to seek employment elsewhere. It'll be difficult since I don't even have a reference from Mr. Twist. Too late to ask him now."

TWENTY SIX

Later Kokk sat alone in the hotel bar, the Elm Water Hole, tasting a Lone Star beer and wondering where Janie was. He'd tried her cell phone without result, even knocked on her room door. No Janie.

He sat at the old fashioned fifty-foot bar alternately staring at a giant mounted elk head above and a stained glass and mirrored backdrop beneath. All the bar room and adjoining pool table walls bore more unblinking stuffed heads of exotic animals.

Kokk shut his eyes briefly, hoping to break their hypnotic spell. "Hope those staring eyes don't haunt my dreams tonight," he groused.

The huge double doors of oak opened as the two pilots from Flight 236 entered the bar. Nodding at Kokk, they joined him at the long polished bar.

Both aviators wore razor-creased fresh uniforms. Kokk saw himself in the bar mirror. He looked like a stained, well-rumpled, around-the-world air traveler.

"Join me in a drink," he invited, offering his hand to one, then the other.

"I'm Jan Kokk. We didn't have a chance to exchange pleasantries in your cockpit where we last met."

"I well remember," Captain Bringuel introduced himself. "Your warning that a bomb aboard the plane might blow us out of the sky was terrifying."

"You certainly captured our full attention, Mr. Kokk. I'm First Officer Benson.

"Where's that cute Janie who accompanied you to the cockpit?"

"Looking for her myself," Kokk smiled, signaling the barkeep for more drinks. "I take it we're not cleared for takeoff to LA yet?"

Both pilots lifted their bottles to toast the big man from Curacao. "How's the investigation going, Mr. Kokk? We heard you're helping the local law."

"I'm just an observer," Kokk wiped his lips. "Is it true that you have an eighteen hour rule about drinking alcohol before flying?"

"True," both pilots answered. "That may prevent our having a drink at the big party being planned for tonight. You're invited, if you haven't heard about it already."

"No, I haven't. Who's the host?"

Bringuel finished his beer. "I think it's a pay-as-you-go bar. Ann and Janie are planning it. So it ought to be a blast."

Benson checked his watch, then motioned for the check. "This bill is mine. Sorry we've got to scurry back to check our plane. It was just inspected by a Southwest team flown here from Dallas."

"*Danki,* gentlemen," Kokk thanked them in Papiamentu, Curacao's dialect.

Bringuel waved as they left the bar. "We'll see you at the party tonight."

Suddenly alone, Kokk picked up a newspaper from the bar. The front-page headline of the *Kerrville Daily Times* read "No Passengers Injured During Emergency Landing At Airport."

Beneath the big thirty-six point head, the story continued. "Due to a bomb hoax, Southwest Flight 236 with 156 passengers plus crew made an emergency landing at the Kerrville-Kerr County Airport yesterday evening.

"Authorities, including the FBI, Texas Rangers and the Kerr County Sheriff Department are investigating the bomb hoax.

"Just before the aircraft landed safely here, the body of a passenger was discovered in a restroom. The name of the deceased has not been released as of press time due to delayed notification of the deceased's next-of-kin.

"In a press conference held at the airport this morning, authorities announced that their investigations of the death, now confirmed as a homicide, as well as the bomb hoax, are in progress."

The blonde bartender answered Kokk's signal by bringing him another Lone Star. She wore Wrangler jeans, boots and a western shirt with ruby snap buttons that matched her lipstick. The shirt was as tight as a Texas sausage casing. On her way back to the kitchen, she turned on the bar's CD player.

Kokk sipped the frosty bottle. A new song. A new singer. I'm acclimating to Texas, he thought.

The singer's name sounded like Wilhelm Nelson and the plaintive song was something about *Blue Eyes Crying in the Rain.*

After several stanzas, Kokk opted for his ear buds and tuned to one of his favorites, *Der Fliegende Hollander.*

The Wagner-provided comfort didn't last long. Someone shook Kokk's shoulder even before the overture ended.

"Mr. Kokk, Mr. Kokk."

Kokk opened his eyes. It was Deputy John Rabe who'd given him a ride to the hotel the previous night.

"Sorry to bother you, sir. But your presence over in building 1 is requested by the big four."

Kokk's quizzical look earned an answer: "You know. The FBI, Texas Ranger, Homeland Security and Sheriff."

Rabe lowered his voice. "They're meeting in a room in the far hotel building and want you there."

In response to the other's "I'll show you the way," Kokk paid his bill and followed Rabe out the double oak doors.

--

Wearily, Consul General Piaker studied his image in the morning mirror. A longish crew cut. receding hair line, watery, squinty eyes and a bulbous red nose returned the look with distaste.

He hadn't slept well last night despite an expensive dinner and drinks with Judy, his dictatorial, scheming but statuesque secretary.

Although she was owed a month's back salary, Judy complained only on weekends. That's when Piaker took her to dinner to assuage his loneliness since losing the wife.

Judy had aroused him at his mammoth desk at closing time the preceding afternoon. "Jeeze, Johan, you looked dead before I poked you awake. Are you all right?"

Without waiting for a response, she had continued in her usual singsong, "Let's go somewhere nice and grab dinner and drinks."

The morning after dinner and drinks, and more drinks, Piaker struggled to his office atop the Nation's Bank building on Wilshire. As he collapsed in his chair, Judy marched in, bearing a tray with two large coffees. She never knocked.

"Here, Johan," she handed him a big styrofoam cup. "Drink this down. You'll feel better."

Wearing a revealing purple sheath and heels, she plopped in the visitor's chair, crossing long legs and blowing on her coffee.

"You remember what you told me last night about the sorry state of your finances?" She asked with the assurance that his memory hadn't survived the previous evening.

He fended, almost spilling coffee. "Not exactly."

"Well, you said," she batted blue eyes at his weak defense. "You said that if you didn't come up with the $30,000 you'd ransacked from the budget, you'll be fired.

"True?"

He shut his eyes and nodded. "Are you sure I said $30,000?"

"You did."

"Whew," he breathed. "I thought Henri, our administrative bean-counter, told me it was more than that."

Judy extended a finger. "That's exactly why you should be listening to me instead of that Judas. He wants your job.

"You know that don't you, Johan?"

Hanging his head, he agreed. "Yes, I know that," he whispered.

Judy stood for emphasis. "I have devised a method for you to extract yourself from this mess you've created. Maybe you could even keep this job."

He raised his head warily. "Why would you care?"

Eyes glinting, she recited her talking points.

"You and I could form a strong partnership for the future, Johan. You continue here in LA until retirement from your government. By then we'd have most of the mortgage paid off on some nice cozy little house in Westwood."

"Whew," he expelled. "What about my wife?"

Judy pointed at him. "She left you here holding the bag, didn't she?

"Well, I'm here and I'm offering you a lifeline!

"You do see that, don't you?"

To his unblinking stare, she repeated. "Don't you see that, Johan?"

TWENTY SEVEN

The afternoon sun had lost some of its brightness and the evening temperature began slowly ebbing. The two men walked out the hotel's front portico past the old-time chuck wagon, then next door to building 1, named 'Bear Creek.'

Kokk called Janie on her cell phone before entering the building. Receiving no response, he left a voice mail.

"I'm at yet another meeting, Janie. I regret each moment away from you, bewitching lady. Don't forget our dinner engagement, *dushi.*"

Another deputy standing guard by room 100 nodded and opened the door for Kokk.

Inside the room sat the senior representatives of their agencies: FBI, Texas Rangers, Homeland Security and Sheriff's Department. Conversation stopped as Kokk entered and took the only vacant chair around a long fold-up table.

Erupting from his chair, Sheriff Swartz knocked it over. "This man has no business here. He has no authority, no accreditation!"

"Sit down, Sheriff," Agent Westbrook raised his voice. "I'm tired of hearing that. Knock it off.

"Mr. Kokk is here at our invitation. We need him since the rest of us appear to be stymied in this investigation.

"We're glad you're here, Mr. Kokk. We value your opinion. Please comment whenever you like."

"Thank you," Kokk smiled grimly, wondering if Janie already had forgotten him. Or was she busy party-planning the evening with Ann?

To relieve tension, Captain Hooks poured himself coffee and pushed the big pot over to the next person. "How about coffee all around?"

The sheriff sat down like a truculent student. "I just want my objections noted by everyone here," he mumbled, accepting a refill of his empty cup.

Westbrook began. "I asked for our meeting here instead of at the airfield to avoid the demands of the reporters out there for another press conference.

"Truth is, we seem to have little in the way of news to tell them and the TV crews. Am I correct?"

The others glumly agreed.

"So this is a session--free of the press and hoopla--to share, to review, what we've developed so far."

Hooks volunteered first. "That residue testing was inconclusive except for Babbs. None of the other tests showed traces of lipstick or strychnine or…. What was his prescription drug called?"

"Digitoxin," Roe from Homeland Security called out.

Kokk held up a hand.

"Yes, Mr. Kokk?"

"Was the aircraft crew tested for residue just like the passengers?"

Hooks responded. "No, we did not test the crew--nor yourself, Mr. Kokk. Recommend we do so?"

Kokk nodded agreement and Hooks made a note.

"I've yet to see any evidence of linkage," the sheriff repeated his theme, "between the bomb hoax and the murder. We have two separate cases here," he insisted.

"Mr. Kokk?"

Kokk cleared his throat. "It's conceivable that a first class passenger walked back to the rear restroom and wrote that bomb threat on the mirror, then returned to his or her seat at the front of the plane.

"That same first class passenger could have substituted poison in the capsules Twist left in the front restroom."

"Why would Twist have taken what he thought was his reserve medication?" challenged the sheriff, chewing on a fresh cigar.

Hooks answered. "Possibly the captain's announcement of an emergency landing so alarmed Twist that he needed extra medication. There it was, quickly available in the restroom."

"And water to take with it," Roe added.

"On that topic," Westbrook joined, "the interviews of the two females indicate that one of them could have dumped the digitoxin out of the capsules left in the restroom and substituted poison." He leaned back in his chair, looking at the others for a response.

"Perhaps Twist felt extremely stressed when he heard the plane was making an emergency landing, He hurriedly took the poison capsules left in the place of the others."

"But which female?" Hooks asked. "They both had the opportunity. What could have been their motive for the poisoning?"

"Right," Swartz took the cigar out of his mouth. "All six of those first class passengers depended on Roger Twist for their bread and butter. Why would any of them want him dead?" He attempted to spit into a nearby wastebasket but missed.

Seeing the sheriff's cigar, Kokk felt in a pocket for his pipe. "Speaking of opportunity, don't forget Robert," he advised, giving up his search.

"We learned from Babbs that Robert also had access to Twist's digitoxin."

"Back to motive," Swartz persisted. "Who gains from Twist's death?

"Or who gains the most?" he growled, clamping down on the cigar.

"*Cui bono?*" Kokk whispered to himself.

Westbrook reacted. "How's that?"

"Sorry," Kokk answered. "I was just musing over the sheriff's point. 'Who gains?' is the classic question to be asked in a murder.

"Perhaps we're overlooking another motive. If it's not money, maybe something in the past of one of the suspects precipitated Twist's murder."

Deputy Rabe knocked, immediately entering the room. "Sorry to interrupt," he wheezed. "But I thought you'd want to know right away that one of the passengers is missing."

"Who?" They asked in unison.

Rabe caught his breath. "That lady in first class. Called Babbs."

Sheriff Swartz jumped up, jubilant. "Case closed!"

TWENTY EIGHT

At Janie's suggestion, she met Kokk outside by the hotel pool. In a blue bikini trimmed in taffeta, she lounged in a deck chair. Kokk claimed a lounge chair beside her.

"I'm breathing like a schoolboy on his first date," he confessed after hugging her.

"You've certainly been avoiding me lately, Mr. Kokk," she said with an impish grin. "I thought you'd forgotten me, just another admiring, doting flight attendant.

"By the way, what's a *dushi?*"

He kissed her hand. "I seriously missed you, lady. There was absolutely no avoidance on my part. The minutes in those meetings I was obliged to attend seemed like hours."

"Don't soft talk me, Mister," she feigned a pout. "I still want to know what's a *dushi?*

"Does it mean you've forsaken me for someone else? Like glamorous Gloria?"

Kokk chuckled. "I know you well enough that you've guessed *dushi* means darling in Papiamentu. What shall we drink to celebrate our finally being together, eye-to-eye?"

"Gin and tonic, but not so fast." She placed her fists on his chest. "I don't even know if you're married and have a dozen little pirates back home in Curacao."

He signaled the bartender tending the Jersey Lilly pool bar. "No to both. You never told me when is that wedding."

"For good reason, curious man. There is no wedding." She teased, "Sure you're not going to run away to another of those strange meetings? What are they all about?"

Kokk studied her, then lifted off her sunglasses. "So I can see those expressive eyes," he said softly.

He changed the subject. "How was your luncheon with Ann and Babbs?"

"She didn't want to go. Said she wasn't feeling well and stayed in her room. The good Samaritan effort was a bust."

Kokk packed his pipe and lit it, watching Janie's expression. "Where is she now?"

"Ann or Babbs?"

"Babbs."

"Probably still in her room. Haven't seen her since she turned down our--your--luncheon idea. Why?"

"You don't know she's missing?"

"Babbs is **missing**?"

"That's the report."

Janie replaced the sunglasses. "Well.... Maybe we should try knocking on her door."

"She's not there. Apparently her room has been cleaned out, luggage and all. Even her toothbrush is gone." Kokk puffed to keep the sailor-cut pipe tobacco glowing.

He patted her cheek with a free hand. "Any idea where she may have gone?"

"No," Janie shook her head emphatically. "Why would I? I wouldn't have hardly known her were it not for your idea of taking her to lunch.

"What's that group of lawmen you've been meeting with think? Does her disappearance make Babbs the lead suspect?"

He finished his drink and wagged at the barman. "The others seem to think so, especially the sheriff. They've sent out what they call an all-points bulletin to alert the law to look for her."

He nudged her. "Wonder what I could read in those marvelous eyes if you took off the sunglasses now?"

She scooted her lounge chair closer and touched his arm. "Then I'm leaving the glasses on. My thoughts might embarrass you, curious corsair."

Kokk handed her the fresh drink. "Speaking of investigating, where were you all day? I tried to call you for hours."

"Ann and I have been out, busy planning our big bash tonight. It took us hours! I must have left my cell phone in the room.

"The party's going to be a doozy. You are taking me, of course?"

She made the question a statement by sitting in his lap and kissing him.

He caught his breath. "Of course. You and Ann are hosting this all on your own?"

93

"No way," she traced his mouth with a little finger. "The airline just sent us a representative with an open checkbook to keep the passengers entertained. Ann and I plan it. The airline pays for it. Crazy, huh?"

Without prompting, Janie outlined the planned mixer and dinner at a local restaurant. "Ann and I thought we'd take the passengers out for a little local color. The buses that brought us here are taking us to Mamacitas, the largest restaurant in town."

She looked doubtfully at Kokk. "We plan on cocktails--that means hefty margaritas—-followed by a huge buffet of Mexican specialties.

"I hope you like fajitas, tacos, enchiladas, tortillas, quesadillas, that sort of thing?"

"Love 'em," Kokk clinked glasses. "When do we leave and is it dressy?"

"Kerrville casual, we're calling it. You and I can leave here in about two hours. Ann's staying behind to get the buses loaded and hustle them to Mamacitas, which is right on the main drag.

"Meanwhile," she indicated the pool, "I'm taking a dip in this beautiful, warm water.

"Join me?"

"I'm not letting you out of my sight until returning you gently to Ann's door tonight. You still room with her?"

"Ask me later." With that she entered the shallow end of the fan-shaped pool and began languidly swimming across the big YO brand displayed on the pool's bottom.

Removing a handkerchief, Kokk gingerly blotted her lipstick on it. He slid the folded cloth back into a pocket, then stood to help her out of the pool.

She giggled. "Stop staring, Jan. I know I look great! And you! You look ravenous."

"As well I should. You remind me of the fabled water nymph."

He kissed her wet face. "I intend devouring you, bit by bit, beautiful princess of air and water.

"Now's…." He started wrapping her in a large beach towel. "Now's the time to tell me all about Janie. For starters, are you engaged? Going steady? I believe those are the current terms."

Janie held his hand. "Let's go to my room. Maybe Ann's out somewhere."

--

"We've looked everywhere for that Babbs female," Sheriff Swartz took the cigar out of his mouth to announce to his assembled colleagues.

"The Kerrville Police Chief volunteered to help my deputies scour the city. We've tried everywhere. Absolutely no sign of that lady."

"Airlines, buses, taxis, other hotels and motels?" Westbrook frowned, thinking the disappearance would require another news conference.

"What about the vacant rooms at the hotel? The dumpsters?"

Ranger Captain Hooks looked solemn. "What about the Guadalupe River that runs through town?"

Swartz repeated. "Everywhere, especially the river. And we've had no reports or tips about her, either."

--

Consul General Piaker stared out his window after Judy left. Autos and trucks down on Wilshire competed in short dashes to the next stoplight. There they sat, roiling engines while waiting for the light to change. The scene always entertained him.

Turning to his desk, he picked up the *Financial Daily* magazine and *Wall Street Journal* left by Judy. She'd yellow-lined two articles for him to read before her return. The articles were a detailed discussion of the recent resurgence of the Mexican peso's value.

The door banged open and a determined Judy strode in.

"You're taking me to lunch," she announced. "Or is your credit card maxed out?

"C'mon," she urged him. "Get up. Put on your coat, I already told Henri we're leaving."

Once on the sidewalk outside the building, she turned and pointed. "How about Grigio's across the street there? They have absolutely great linguine."

He followed her lead, thoughts full of their--rather, her--previous conversation. He remained baffled by the finality, the intensity, of her proposal. Did she really expect him to leave his wife and become a California suburbanite?

Once seated in the small restaurant, he ordered the wine, attempting to restore their boss-secretary roles.

Her eyes glowed over the rim of her wineglass. "Did you read those articles I left you?"

He cleared his throat. "Yes, I scanned them."

"And?"

"Most interesting but I don't see their application to my career. You do know that some kind of officer from Willemstad is on his way here, to escort me back to Curacao? I'm to face the wrath--I presume--of my uncle, our most excellent Foreign Minister."

"Of course, I know that. I'm here to restore you, to help you make money, big money," she gestured.

"You **can** get back on your feet, Johan. Tell your uncle that the shortages were the result of your administrative officer's negligence."

"Make big money?" he repeated.

"How?" he asked as their salads were served

She raised her eyes upward. "Haven't you been listening? Read those articles. There's plenty of opportunity if you invested in Mexican pesos. Forecasters say the peso will go through the ceiling."

He swallowed. "I must have missed that."

She held out her hand. "Give me your pen, Johan."

She began writing on the mat pulled from beneath her plate. "Look here," she pointed toward the numbers she'd scrawled.

"The current price of the peso is 12.3 per dollar. It's expected to raise to 13.7 by the end of this month and to hit 14, maybe even 15 next month."

Palms raised, he pleaded. "You know I have no money."

"But your consulate account at the bank does."

Shaking his head, he muttered, "There's not much left. And it's not mine to dabble with. The ministry might even freeze the account soon."

"Not if you show the ministry that the account's growing."

"Growing?" he blinked. "How?"

She sighed. "By exchanging all the dollars in the account into pesos! Then you sit back and watch the profits grow as the peso appreciates! That's how!"

Judy selected a fork and spoon. "Let that sink in. The linguine's getting cold. Then we'll talk."

TWENTY NINE

Ann stood in the lead vehicle as the caravan of passenger-filled buses entered the parking lot of Mamacitas restaurant. The building sat between two thoroughfares near the middle of town. The restaurant epitomized Spanish colonial architecture. Tall towers framed a gold dome. Beneath the dome was a portico entrance with an emblazoned **BIENVENIDOS** welcome.

Colored lights sparkled in the adjoining flower garden surrounding a small pool. Inside the entrance was a high ceiling waiting area. A large, circular crystal candelabra hung from the ceiling.

The first entrance door was held open by Kokk. The second by Janie, welcoming passengers trailing Ann through the waiting area.

Facing them as they entered a larger room was a mural depicting the famous Alamo mission in San Antonio where Travis' Texans were overwhelmed by the Mexican army.

Beside the foyer a quartet of musicians wearing Mexican *charro* outfits entertained with *mariachi* music.

In the party room to the right hurried waitresses offering margarita drinks of tequila and lime. Above the clink of glasses, the conversations all concerned Babbs, the missing passenger.

"Who is she?"
"Where could she be?"
"Does this mean she murdered that man?"
"I don't remember her."
"I think she sat up front with that Hollywood group."
"Maybe she's that movie actress?"

--

The noise level had risen so high that Kokk leaned forward to speak in Ann's ear.

"Congratulations for organizing this soiree," he began, almost spilling his drink. "You and Janie must have worked all afternoon on this."

"Is your question the preface to a grope?" she teased. "Or are you just curious?"

Giving her a pat, he countered. "Would your answers be different?"

Ann winked. "Answer one is get rid of your room mate and we'll talk about it later.

"Answer two is it took us barely an hour to wrap up the whole thing. Mamacitas management handled everything for us.

"Why do you ask?"

"Just wondering," Kokk handed her a drink from the tray of a passing waitress. "Just wondering."

Someone tapped on a glass for attention. It was Janie, standing in the middle of the room beside a stranger in business suit and tie.

"That's the airline rep sent here to calm our passengers," Ann whispered in Kokk's ear.

Janie began, once the noise quieted. "May I introduce Mr. Fred Reed, representing the home office of Southwest Airline, the generous host of tonight's get-together. He's flown here from Dallas to assure that we're well cared for in Kerrville."

Muted cheers.

"Mr. Reed has a very important announcement which concerns us all. Mr. Reed."

A loud voice bellowed from the back of the room. "When do we leave?" Other voices reinforced the question.

Waving his hand, Reed acknowledged the question. "On the behalf of Southwest, I apologize for this unavoidable delay and the unfortunate incident requiring the emergency landing.

"Needless to say, we deeply regret the loss of a passenger upon completion of that emergency landing.

"As you know, we sought to make your stay-over here as comfortable as possible by providing you lodging and meals in one of the city's finest hotels.

"As to your question about leaving, the law enforcement authorities with whom I've just spoken indicate that we may resume our flight to Los Angeles sometime tomorrow.

"The 'may' word is contingent upon the successful conclusion of the investigations about the bomb hoax and the untimely death of one of our passengers."

Loud applause and cheers drowned out Reed's next words and he had to start again once the clapping had subsided.

"Those same authorities are asking our help in locating a passenger missing since this morning from the hotel. The missing lady is Ms. Babbs Solomon, about whom we are deeply concerned.

"If any of you saw Ms. Solomon this morning or know where she might be, please tell one of the uniformed officers at the back of the room. They will be here for the entire evening. If you have any information about Ms. Solomon and her whereabouts, please share it with one of the officers.

"Enjoy the evening. The buses will remain in the parking lot for the remainder of the evening. Their last trip back to our hotel will be at midnight.

"On behalf of Southwest, we appreciate your selecting us as your air carrier and hope you will choose to fly Southwest on your very next trip. Thank you."

As Reed stepped aside, Janie led the applause, then announced the buffet lines were open. Breathless, she rejoined Ann and Kokk as they stood, watching the others form lines about the buffet serving stations.

FBI Agent Daniels paused beside Kokk as people began queuing for the buffet. "Your tip paid off," he shook Kokk's hand.

In answer to Kokk's puzzled look, Daniels explained. "You said we should bear down on Robert, that 'go-fer' guy. We did and he came clean about that letter Twist found in his plane seat."

"What happened?"

"Seems Robert picked up Twist's mail at their hotel in Sao Paulo as they left for the airport."

Kokk shook his head in amusement. "I'm guessing that Robert forgot to give Twist the letter until they got on the plane to LA. On that flight, he dropped the letter in Twist's chair while Twist was in the restroom 'conferring' with Gloria."

Kokk smiled broadly as Daniels continued to nod agreement. "Twist's reaction on reading the threat letter badly frightened Robert. He was afraid to confess that he had neglected to deliver it earlier, later that he placed the letter on Twist's chair."

"Right you are, Mr. Kokk. Do you read minds, too?"

"And I bet that threatening letter was unmarked, except for Twist's name."

"Right again." Daniels found himself a niche in the buffet line. "Just thought you'd like to know."

Kokk waved as he joined Janie and Ann searching for a table. "Many thanks, Agent Daniels."

A tipsy Louisa, the senior flight attendant, stopped in front of Janie, whom she google-eyed.

"I see you're hoggin' the microphone, again, Melanie from Cleveland. Is that something you and Vicky saw on that TV show?" She guffawed and walked away, almost tripping.

Ann grabbed Janie's arm. "Don't even think about what you're thinking about. Forget her. Let's find us a good table." Ann aimed Janie at a nearby table, grabbing Kokk by the sleeve.

Moon and Gloria sat alone at a large table. Moon motioned for the trio to join them.

Gloria sniffed as Kokk seated Ann and Janie. He eyed Gloria speculatively.

Making a face at Kokk, Gloria began a monologue as if Kokk was questioning her.

"Yes, Babbs is my roommate.

"No, I don't know where she is.

"I last saw her when I went to bed last night.

"Haven't seen her since," Gloria firmly concluded, turning to Moon to light her cigarette.

Janie studied the starlet. "Must be troubling for you," she said softly.

"What?"

"Well, you might be the last person to see Roger Twist alive. Maybe you were the last to see Babbs, too.

Janie turned to Kokk. "Quite a coincidence, don't you think?

"You even might be labeled a serial.... Now what is that term?"

"Why, you, you viper!" Gloria stood screaming, attempting to slap Janie.

"How dare you insinuate that I was responsible?" she shrieked, ignoring the shocked buffet diners behind her.

"Get me out of here, Harold! Now!

"I won't stand for this kind of abuse from a... a...." Gloria left the sentence unfinished as she grabbed Moon by the arm and pulled him toward the door.

"I'm on her like a chicken on a June bug," Janie chortled. "Don't you agree, Jan? She must be your group's number one suspect."

Without a word, Kokk began filling his pipe.

"Now we've vacated two chairs at our table," she motioned to Perry and Oliver, silently standing there to join them.

Pleased with herself, she stood, looking to Ann, then at Kokk. "Maybe we should join the buffet lines now that they're shorter? I'm famished."

THIRTY

"I'm constantly amazed by you," Kokk whispered in her ear as they sat beside the YO swimming pool after returning on the last bus. From his hotel room Kokk had brought his habitual traveling companion, a squat bottle of cognac.

He half-filled the glasses borrowed from the bartender closing the wet bar. He handed Janie one.

"How so, lover?" Janie uncoiled an arm about his neck to accept the glass.

Kokk splayed his hands toward the sky. "What am I going to do with you?"

"Love me. Idolize me," she answered. "You can manage both, can't you?"

Kokk grinned so widely his white teeth glistened. "You've yet to tell you about yourself. Here I am, a foundering older man, wanting--no--demanding to know everything about you."

"Persistent, aren't you?" she fended. "I think you have a background fetish of some kind. Must come from your dubious occupation."

She neatly reversed their roles. "Which is what, Jan? What exactly do you do down there in sunny Curacao?"

He packed and lit the pipe. "I invite you to visit. I'd like to show you first-hand and personal what I do."

"Maybe."

"I'm hoping to prompt your confession by my own. I'm a private investigator. No wife. No family.

"I live in Willemstad, capital of the fair island of Curacao. If you visited once, you'd never leave. It's that lovely.

"I left it briefly as a youngster. I'd been a local policeman and volunteered for training in the Royal Dutch Gendarmerie in the Netherlands.

"I served there several years until I was wounded in Surinam and invalided-out of service. So, I returned home to Willemstad and opened my own investigation office.

"Practice is pretty good. Lots of background investigations," he blinked at her, "divorces, missing people, traces and such.

"There," he puffed repeatedly to keep the pipe aglow. "Now I expect to hear **your** life history."

Janie sighed and leaned back in his arms. "So your wound is responsible for that limp I've noticed?"

"Yes. Life history," he demanded. "Your turn."

"Is this really necessary? My history's a bore, even to me."

"Let's hear it," he insisted.

"I grew up in Shamrock, in the Texas Panhandle. My mother worked at the local bank as long as I can remember. She finally retired shortly before she passed.

"I never knew my father, Apparently Mother didn't know him well, either. Either that or she's shielded me from who or what he was for reasons of her own.

"I couldn't afford college after high school so I worked odd jobs around town for a year."

Remembering something, Janie sat up. "I answered an airlines advertisement for training to become what was then called an air hostess. I enjoy the work and travel, I do it well.

"Haven't had the time nor interest in marrying yet. I used to visit my mother as often as flight scheduling allowed. Ann and I share a small townhouse in Dallas."

"Thus your Texas brogue," Kokk touched her lip with his little finger.

"Thus my Shamrock, Texas brogue," she grunted, nipping the finger.

"You know nothing about your father?"

"Only what I've scrounged from one of those ancestry services. He left mother before my birth. She hadn't heard from him for twenty or thirty years."

Kokk nodded. "But you have."

She squirmed in the adjoining lounge chair. "That didn't sound like a question."

"It wasn't."

"Maybe I should hire you, Mister PI, to locate my long lost father."

"I could do that," he agreed. "That way I'd always know how to immediately contact his beautiful, charming, suddenly nervous daughter."

"Do we agree?" she asked, finishing her drink.

"Absolutely."

"Your room or mine?"

--

After lunch, Judy guided Piaker into the bank entrance. "Remember what I told you to say?"

"Of course, I remember," he frowned. "But making money from pesos can't be this easy. Everybody'd be doing it."

They were escorted to the desk of a smiling bank officer. Johan identified himself and the reason for their visit. "I want to exchange all the US dollars in the Consulate account into Mexican pesos immediately."

The officer studied them. "Of course, that's possible. I hope you aren't planning on transferring your account elsewhere?"

Piaker smiled. "No, not at all. You've been our bank since the Consulate was established here twelve years ago."

"And you've been a superb client, sir." The officer made a notation on his screen and passed Johan a just-printed paper to sign, formalizing the exchange to pesos.

"I can access account balances on the telephone or on the computer as before?"

"Certainly, sir."

With that they left the bank and returned to the elevators. Judy hugged him. "Congratulations, Johan! Now you're on the way to making big bucks!

Johan shook his head in disbelief. "Do you really think this will work? We should celebrate!"

THIRTY ONE

The desk clerk rang Kokk's new, just acquired room in the YO Hotel early the next morning.

"Sorry to disturb you at this early hour, sir. A deputy sheriff is looking for you with a message. He didn't find you in your regular room and I felt obliged to give him your present room number. The deputy is on his way to you now with the message.

"Thought I'd call and alert you. Again, I apologize for disturbing."

Janie rolled over. "What is it, Jan?"

"A deputy is coming here with a message. It's probably about another one of those meetings they like me to attend.

"No need for you to squirm," he assured her. "I'll take the message at the door."

She rose up on one elbow. "Damn! I can't compete with another one of your meetings? Even after last night?"

Kokk put on trousers and opened the door at the deputy's knock. The spoken message was that his presence was requested at an immediate meeting in building 1.

"Thanks," Kokk said without enthusiasm. "I'll be there. At least I don't have to go all the way to the airport," he scowled, reaching for the telephone to order a pot of coffee.

She sat up in bed covered by a YO embossed sheet. "I can't believe you're going to leave me like this," she pouted.

"Hot coffee does not make amends, Jan Kokk. Why must **you** attend these meetings? Are you being paid for your wisdom and advice?"

"Hardly." He searched on the bureau for tip money.

"I'm very upset that you're deserting me. I might as well have spent the night with Ann in my own room."

Kokk took the coffee tray at the door in exchange for the tip. He set the tray down carefully and filled two cups.

"On the other hand," he studied her wake-up face and graded it marvelous, "I have absolutely no regrets about last night. You know I'll be back just as soon as I can.

"Don't you?"

Janie tasted the steaming coffee. "This meeting sure as hell clouds what I thought might be our…future."

She looked near tears. "Presuming we had one."

He cradled her face, kissing her eyelids. "First you're feisty," he chuckled. "Now you're weepy. Which is my real Janie?"

He kissed her, stilling an answer. Grinning at her confusion, he tried reassurance.

"We absolutely have a future, delightful, sweet Janie. We'll work it out as soon as I get back from this meeting, hopefully my last."

She held up a small hand, like a schoolgirl. "You know what that Southwest rep said last night? Our flight may resume today."

She buried her head in a pillow. "You and I haven't much time together.

"And you're spending what little time we have for ourselves **in another damn meeting!"**

--

Another deputy nodded, offered an envelope and held open the door to room 100, building 1, 'Bear Creek.'

Kokk accepted the envelope as he rubbed the stubble on his chin. Shaving while Janie lounged in their bed would have been a terrible waste of time, he thought. He took a chair in the back row, next to two agents from the FBI team.

The assembled officials from FBI, Rangers, Sheriff Department and Kerrville Police were busily attempting to drain a huge urn of hot coffee. Roe, of Homeland Security, had apparently returned to Washington, Kokk decided. He shook his head when offered coffee. Instead, he opened the envelope.

It was a report from the technician who examined the lipstick smear on Kokk's handkerchief.

Reading the report, Kokk suppressed a groan. He folded the report and pocketed it.

Captain Hooks signaled he'd like to see Kokk later.

Disturbed by the report just handed him, Kokk's thoughts wandered to Janie. Will she still be in our room when I return? My next coffee--or whatever the beverage--must be with her.

Agent-in-Charge Westbrook sat at a large table beside Texas Ranger Captain Hooks and Sheriff Swartz. As usual, the sheriff glared at Kokk.

"The purpose of this short meeting," Westbrook began, "is to outline our program, supplemented by your suggestions, for today.

"We announced to the press and TV crews still here that we'd hold a second press conference at the hotel at 10:00 a.m. this morning.

"The hotel is kindly allowing us to use the adjoining Live Oak and Cypress rooms for this purpose. As I came here from breakfast, the press is already setting up equipment in those rooms.

"I intend that this press briefing be shorter than our previous one at the airport. However we can expect just as many, if not more, questions

"Are we ready?" Westbrook asked, pushing his chair back to stand.

--

Kokk trailed the others into the YO's conference rooms to meet the assembled TV crews and reporters. Westbrook stood behind the table separating the officials from the audience. Hooks and Swartz took chairs beside Westbrook.

Looking about the audience, Westbrook nodded to several reporters, then began speaking.

"I have three major points I intend to cover today. First, our investigations into the bomb hoax and the murder of a passenger are continuing. The investigations are neither delayed nor ceasing. They are continuing.

"Second. A person of interest--to use the popular TV term--has been identified. That person is a passenger on Flight 236 whom we are attempting to locate as we speak.

"Ms. Barbara (Babbs) Solomon, has been missing from her hotel room since yesterday morning when her absence was reported. A national all-points bulletin or BOLO has been issued to expedite our location of this lady. With her assistance, we hope to wrap up our investigation of the two criminal acts: the bomb hoax and the murder.

"Third. In view the above, Flight 236 may resume travel to its destination as soon as airline officials desire. The passengers and their baggage will be returned to the airport and normally processed by the airline. They will then board the same airplane, which has been repeatedly searched and prepared for safe flight.

"The airline will announce the departure time to passengers at the hotel as soon as we end this conference.

"I would be extremely remiss as we end this conference if I failed to commend the following individuals and agencies for their outstanding efforts and contributions to our team efforts to conclude this case.

"Please stand, Captain of the Texas Rangers Hooks and his Ranger team." Hooks and his Rangers stood momentarily, followed by scattered applause from the audience.

"Sheriff Swartz and his department have worked this case tirelessly and continuously since the emergency landing of Flight 236. Please stand, Sheriff and deputies."

More applause.

"Now I'd like my FBI teammates to stand, please. We came to Kerrville unfamiliar with your community and facilities. The cooperation extended us by the Texas Rangers, the Sheriff Department and Kerrville Police has been first-rate." Uneven applause followed.

"We sincerely appreciate the efforts of the Kerrville Police which have played an essential role in traffic control and searching the city for the missing passenger. Thank you very much.

"Finally, I want to recognize the valuable assistance given our investigators by a gentleman who happened to be a passenger on Flight 236. He is a private detective from Curacao and performing a mission for his government when the plane made its emergency landing here in Kerrville. Please stand, Mr. Kokk.

"Mr. Kokk, an experienced investigator, was an immediate and valuable resource since he personally witnessed the events on the airplane. Your observations and advice gave our investigators a running start. Thank you, Mr. Kokk."

Reporters turned to study the big man now standing in the rear row.

Sheriff Swartz glowered as several reporters and officers applauded.

"We will take your questions now."

Immediately, hands filled the air.

Westbrook pointed to a *Kerrville Daily Times* reporter in the first row. "Since an all-points bulletin has been issued to locate…"

Westbrook affirmed the reporter's last word with a nod.

The reporter continued, "this person. Would you repeat her name?"

"Her name is Ms. Barbara, nickname, Babbs, last name Solomon. Her home is listed as Westwood, California."

"Is she suspected of writing the bomb message in the restroom?"

"Until we interview the lady, we have no comment."

"Did Ms. Solomon know Mr. Twist, the deceased?"

"She was his personal secretary."

A San Antonio reporter raised both hands.

"Yes?"

"If you are allowing the other passengers to resume travel, does that mean Ms. Solomon is suspected of the bomb hoax as well as the murder?"

Westbrook rubbed his nose. "No comment until we have a chance to interview the lady."

Another hand, from another questioner, went up. "Have you identified a possible motive for the murder?"

"Sorry, no comment at this time."

A TV commentator wagged his hand. "In your opinion was the bomb hoax and the murder committed by one person or several?"

"We're still developing leads," Westbrook replied crisply.

Suddenly the angry sheriff spoke up. "In my opinion, there is no connection between the two crimes."

"We're still developing leads," Westbrook repeated, staring down the sheriff.

On that note, Westbrook ended the press conference with a curt "That's all, thank you for coming."

Another reporter called out, "Will there be other announcements? Where do we get progress reports?"

"The FBI agent-in-charge of the Dallas office will coordinate future news releases with the Rangers and the Sheriff Department. Remember, our investigation is continuing. Thank you!"

--

Kokk stepped over to Ranger Captain Hooks as the press crowd left the room. "You wanted to see me?"

"Sure do, Mr. Kokk. You plan to leave on Flight 236, don't you?"

"I certainly hope so. I've neglected my government's assignment too long. I hope it will understand why I am delayed in escorting one of our diplomats back home."

"Maybe this will help," Hooks handed him a thick envelope. "Read it later. It's an attempt of the Texas Rangers to express our gratitude to your government for your assistance in this case. Hopefully it fully explains the reasons for your delay here.

"Agent Westbrook says a similar letter of commendation is on the way to Curacao from the FBI. We were afraid we'd miss you in your haste to get out of here.

"Thank you for every thing, Mr. Kokk, It was a pleasure to meet and work with you. I hope you'll return to Texas and look me up at Ranger headquarters in Austin."

Kokk almost blushed. "You exaggerate my minor contributions, sir. I sincerely thank you. If I miss him, please give my thanks to Agent Westbrook. I wish you both the very best and invite you to visit me in lovely Curacao."

THIRTY TWO

A few minutes later, Kokk impatiently keyed the door to his occupied-the-night-before room.

"Tell me you're still here," he called out as he unlocked the door.

"I'm here, Jan," robed, she sat in an easy chair, reading a newspaper. She grabbed him and kissed his unshaven chin. "You knew damn well I'd wait, didn't you?"

"I hoped. I prayed."

She chuckled. "Jan Kokk prays? There's so much about you I want to know."

Suddenly serious, he asked, "Have you had breakfast?"

"No, love. I was waiting for you." She bussed him again as he pulled her onto his lap.

"Let's have breakfast here in the room," he suggested, still solemn. "There's so much I must say to you and so little time."

"What's the rush? I just heard our flight doesn't depart until 3:00 this afternoon."

He was already on the telephone ordering breakfast from room service. Then he held a chair for her. Once she was seated, he sat down opposite her.

Puzzled, she sat erect. "Why are we being so formal?"

He took a deep breath, studying her. "What I'm about to say--to ask--is of life long impact for both of us.

"I've wrestled with what to say--how to say it--for some time. You've mesmerized the implacable Jan Kokk, who loves you more than he imagined possible."

She grinned and relaxed. "And I love you, mysterious man of my life. Sounds like a big surprise announcement coming up."

Their breakfast arrived on a pushcart. Kokk met the waiter at the door and wheeled it into the room.

He resumed his seat. "You're right, Janie. A big surprise. I've been practicing this for the past few hours. Let me say it all before you react.

"Here goes. Your lipstick and the lipstick on the restroom mirror matched. You wrote that bomb threat, didn't you?"

Janie's face froze. She couldn't speak.

"You even went forward with me to tell the captain the message, knowing he'd declare an emergency."

She lurched forward. "You just open a can of crazy? Stop it, Jan! This isn't funny!"

Ignoring the breakfast before them, Kokk continued. "You must have thought the emergency landing would so frighten Roger Twist that he'd have to take his blood pressure capsules.

"Capsules that you'd emptied into the lavatory, refilled with poison and replaced over the restroom door."

Hand shaking, she poured herself a cup of coffee. After a sip, she lit a cigarette, staring at Kokk. "I'd planned a far different morning with you," she drew deeply.

"Continue."

Kokk poured himself coffee, watching her. "I'm uncertain why you wanted Twist dead. Mind telling me?"

"I'm not confessing to anything, Mr. Inquisitor, except to your lunacy!"

Kokk refilled his pipe and lit it, still studying her. "Twist was your father, wasn't he?" The match burned Kokk's fingers before he could fan it out.

"The FBI file on you isn't complete but that's my guess. He deserted your mother before your birth. He left her destitute while he went to California to seek his fortune. Once you were able, you changed your name to Roland, your mother's maiden name."

"This is completely ridiculous. You just can't control that clever investigator impulse can you?

"What's come over you, Jan? You're destroying the feelings I had for you!"

Kokk repeated. "He left your mother destitute. Although you never knew him as a child, you vowed to find him and get payback for all your mother's suffering."

She stubbed out the cigarette and stood. "I've had enough of this. I'm leaving now."

He held up a hand. "I completely understand your animus toward Twist, Janie. Please let me finish before you decide to run and hide."

She snarled, "Did you call the cops already? Are they outside ready to handcuff me and lead me away?

"My mother died penniless and desperately ill. I'll never forget her suffering. I wanted to make **him** suffer as well and …"

Unable to finish her thought, she sat down, crying and covering her face with a breakfast napkin.

He went to her side and attempted to hold her.

"Don't touch me!" she screamed. "I thought you would be my… my life partner!"

"I intend to be just that," Kokk wiped her tears with the same handkerchief returned with the lab report.

"Let me finish. What did you do with Babbs? You thought her disappearance would end the investigation. All those lawmen would think Babbs ran away to avoid being charged with the hoax and murder. Right?

"What did you do with Babbs?" he repeated.

Her coughing and sobbing prevented speaking for minutes. Finally, composed, she stared at Kokk and lit another cigarette.

She wiped her red eyes again. "I didn't hurt her if that's what you think. She was so distraught by that interrogation that she was sure she'd be arrested. I encouraged her to run away."

New weeping erupted. "Just wish I'd gone with her.

"Yes, I helped her get away early that morning before anyone was up."

"What exactly did you do?"

"I rented a car from the place across from the hotel early that morning. Then I picked up Babbs and her luggage and drove her to the city bus station. I wore her big head scarf, dark raincoat and sunglasses while I bought a ticket for her. She crouched in the back seat of the rental so she wouldn't be seen.

"Waiting for the bus, we traded clothing. Wearing the scarf, raincoat and dark glasses, she could pass for me, the identically dressed woman who had just purchased the bus ticket.

"I knew there was an early bus from Kerrville direct to Del Rio, Texas, on the Mexican border.

"She went there to begin a new life, Jan, far from Hollywood and all that tinsel. If Babbs felt threatened by the law, she could simply walk across the international bridge and start over again in Mexico."

"How much money did you give her?"

She wiped her eyes again. "Oh, she had plenty from her life savings and Twist's travel account. Money was no problem."

Kokk sat back, seeing their untouched breakfast for the first time. "I'm relieved you helped that poor woman," he sighed.

"You have no recriminations about her being suspected of--likely charged--for a murder **you** committed?"

Janie looked offended. "Sure. That bothers me. But understand this," she shook her finger at him. "I have no regrets about Twist.

"What about you, famous investigator? How do you rationalize harboring me, a fugitive? Isn't that what it's called?"

She frowned. "Didn't you take an oath somewhere to uphold law and order? How will you be able to sleep after breaking that oath?"

Kokk replied softly. "Every moment we're apart, I'm deprived, suffering."

His voice cracked. "I'm in pain. I decided being with you is worth whatever I have to relinquish."

He sat looking at his hands, then at her. "I'd like you to write out a confession for Twist's murder."

"You're crazy!" She began sobbing again and hitting him on the chest.

"Hear me out, *dushi*. I'll give your confession to the sheriff after you've gone. That'll absolve Babbs and ease your conscience as well."

"I'll go to prison! Is that what you want? I thought you wanted us to be together!"

"I do. But first I want you to follow Babbs to Del Rio. Reassure her that she's not a suspect.

"Eventually the law will stop looking for a young, attractive airlines attendant. It certainly won't look for her in Del Rio, Texas. But first we must get you on that bus as smoothly as you did Babbs."

She shook her head sadly. "What in the world would I do in Del Rio, Texas?"

Kokk drew another deep breath. "Give it time. If your feelings for me--for our life together--are real, then come to me in Curacao."

Mystified, she leaned forward in his face. "Knowing what I did, how can you love me?"

"Easy, that's how. Why else would I be sitting here beside you, planning your escape?"

He smiled. "Get packed. I'm off to the rental agency for a car. Wear a disguise as you did with Babbs.

"I'll meet you behind this building and drive you to the bus station. Or to San Antonio, if you prefer.

"While I'm gone, write a simple confession. Just a few words. No details."

--

Jubilant, Judy descended to the mall beauty shop where she had her hair shampooed and nails done. Then she purchased a bottle of champagne and a carton of fresh strawberries for an impromptu celebration upstairs with Johan.

She stored the purchases in the office refrigerator, then walked through the open door to Johan's office.

A shaken Henri stood there, staring. "Good God! You're back!"

"Who else?" she countered. "Where's Johan?"

Henri gripped the side of a chair before speaking. "I thought you'd gone with him."

"Gone?"

"You really don't know? Our esteemed Consul emptied our account at the bank an hour ago. The bank called to advise me."

Judy frowned. "What's going on? Where's Johan?"

Exasperated, Henri pointed at her. "Don't you get it? He took all the money in the bank and skipped to Mexico.

"He's probably in Ensenada by now, sipping a margarita and having a big laugh on both of us."

Judy slumped into a chair. "I can't believe this!"

Henri took the big chair behind the desk. "I just spoke to the Ministry in Willemstad. They can't believe it, either.

"Since I presumed you had absconded with Johan, I typed a letter of instruction which the Ministry dictated. Now I'm off to the airport to deliver it to Jan Kokk."

"Who?"

"The man flying here this afternoon to escort Johan back to Curacao. This letter instructs Kokk to return to Curacao immediately without our beloved Consul.

"By the way," Henri chuckled. "You're looking at Curacao's new Consul General. Me! They appointed me to succeed Johan. I'm your boss now."

She studied him, then smiled breathlessly, crossing her legs. "Congratulations, Henri. Richly deserved.

"Now hurry back from your airport delivery and we'll go to supper. I know a great little place where the linguine's simply devine!"

THIRTY THREE

He hardly recognized Janie wearing a dark coat, beret and sunglasses as she crawled into the passenger seat of the Taurus he'd just rented from Enterprise. He leaned forward for a long breathless kiss.

"This is the hardest thing I've ever done in my life," he murmured, passing her a thick hotel envelope.

"Inside are my mailing and email addresses, a repeat of my cell and telephone numbers plus enough cash for a ticket to Curacao--or where ever you choose to go."

She grinned impishly. "You'd better be ready to meet me at your Curacao airport on a moment's notice, Jan Kokk."

"*Di nada,*" he kissed her nose. "It means 'with pleasure.' Better learn a little Papiamentu," he joked to ease the tension.

She directed him to turn right onto a smaller street. In a minute, she nodded at the bus station sitting back off the road.

"Better turn in over there," she pointed to a barbecue restaurant on the opposite corner. "You'd better not be seen driving me to the bus station."

"Nonsense," he murmured. "I'm going inside to buy your ticket."

"No, Jan. No! Then you're implicated in my disappearance. I'll buy it and immediately board the bus there," she pointed again.

"This is sheer torture, letting you walk away."

She kissed him, then slid out the car door. "*Te otro biaha,*" she whispered, quickly walking away with her carry-on.

Shaking his head, Kokk wiped his eyes. Where did she learn that Papiamentu phrase? he asked himself.

"Until next time," he repeated huskily.

--

Holding his first-class boarding pass in one hand, Kokk stopped in front of Sheriff Swartz standing beside the aircraft.

"*Bon tardi.* Here's your receipt, Sheriff. Where are my pistol and passport?"

Without a word the sheriff handed him a package. "They're both in here."

Stooping, Kokk placed the package in his big leather valise. He limped briskly to the waiting airplane.

On his way to the airport, he had intended handing Swartz the short confession penned by Janie. Something in the sheriff's manner caused him to change his mind.

He pocketed her confession and, whistling, boarded the airplane without a backward look.

-end-